Francie

Meet Francie Nelson, delightful, contradictory and spoiled, and not very eager to exchange her gay life at home for goodness-knows-what in post-war England, the "Land of Austerity." And when she was just about to become Beauty Queen too!

" 'Is *this* London?' she demanded in disgust and disappointment. 'Oh, it's horrid. So dull!' " But even the gloom in which Francie luxuriates has its spots of cheer. There's always the fascinating question of English boys—what will they be like?—and, glory be! there's Pop's promise of a fur coat if she sees the year through.

Francie's experience with "hands across the sea" goes far beyond her sack-like school uniform and the lack of central heating. Jennifer's puzzling hostility, the dateless vacations and brisk runs before breakfast are bad enough, but even worse is the hurt of sometimes actually feeling in the wrong just because she was born in America.

Francie and England quarrel and make up a hundred times in that eventful year, and in the end impetuous Francie gets far more than that promised fur coat.

This TEMPO BOOKS *edition contains the complete text of the original hard-cover edition, published by Franklin Watts, Inc., at $2.95*

TEMPO BOOKS

T1—FRANCIE, *by Emily Hahn*
T2—QUEST OF THE SNOW LEOPARD,
    by Roy Chapman Andrews
T3—MOONFLEET, *by J. Meade Falkner*
T4—TRYST, *by Elswyth Thane*
T5—NATIONAL VELVET, *by Enid Bagnold*
T6—INVADERS OF EARTH, *edited by Groff Conklin*
T7—WONDERS OF THE WORLD, *by Leonard Cottrell*
T8—WINNING PITCHER, *by Mark Porter*
T9—MYSTERY OF SATELLITE 7, *by Charles Coombs*
T10—THE RED CAR, *by Don Stanford*
T11—STAR-SPANGLED SUMMER, *by Janet Lambert*
T12—MAGGIE, *by Vivian Breck*

    You will find the same absorbing reading and
high quality in future TEMPO BOOKS. Look
for them wherever books are sold.

TEMPO BOOKS EDITORIAL ADVISORY BOARD

ROBERT F. BEAUCHAMP, *Assistant Professor of English*
    Illinois State Normal University

DONALD CARLINE, *Associate Professor of Education*
    Director, The Reading Center
    Kansas State Teachers College

JERRY E. REED, *Supervisor of English*
    Denver, Colorado, Public Schools

Francie

BY EMILY HAHN

BOOKS

Grosset & Dunlap

NEW YORK

COPYRIGHT 1951 BY EMILY HAHN

TEMPO BOOKS EDITION, 1962
BY ARRANGEMENT WITH FRANKLIN WATTS, INC.

FIRST PRINTING, SEPTEMBER 1962

PRINTED IN THE UNITED STATES OF AMERICA

Francie

CHAPTER 1

THE WHOLE WORLD was white, save for the road where they had parked. The moon had just set but the fields and hedges were still dim and greenish under the darkening sky. Snow covered the ground on either side of the car and made the trees soft and plump. The road was sharply black between the banks, and water, freezing again after a slight thaw, gleamed in puddles along the ruts.

Francie stared through the misty windshield and sighed. She cuddled her chin into the collar of her coat and spoke to the boy behind the wheel. "I hate to think of it, Glenn," she said. "Months and months more of this."

"What's wrong with this?" Glenn Stevens demanded. "Winter's swell; there isn't nearly so much doing in the summer. All the shows come out to Chicago soon. We'll get in for some of them. And we've had a lot of good skating already."

"I just don't like cold weather. Some day," said

Francie dreamily, "I'll go and settle down in Florida, or some South Sea isle. That's better, come to think of it—Tahiti. Wouldn't you like Tahiti, Glenn?"

"I like Jefferson in the wintertime," said Glenn staunchly. "I guess I like the Middle West. Always been glad to get back after a trip away."

"Lucky you, never yearning for what you can't have. How can you ever bring yourself to leave it, and go to State next fall?"

He chose to ignore the mockery in her voice; he answered simply. "That's easy; *you're* going to State. The whole gang's going, almost. If it wasn't that I knew you'd be there, I wouldn't be so keen on college. Not that Dad would let me quit," he added as an afterthought. "I've got to go somewhere, he says, and that's flat. But I'm not like you, Francie, I like Jefferson well enough to stay right here—so long as you're here too." He looked at her, peering in the dark and frowning at a thought which had assailed him. "You haven't told me finally about Prom, by the way," he said.

"Haven't I?" Francie looked in the opposite direction and spoke with an artificial lightness.

"You know darn well you haven't. What about it? Are you coming?"

"Bill asked me yesterday," she said very softly, so softly she nearly whispered. It was one of her most appealing, most unexpected little mannerisms.

The boy sat up straight and Francie stole a look

at him in the faint light from the dashboard. Glenn wasn't the handsomest boy in her crowd, perhaps, but she liked the solid look of him. He was more grown up than any of the others, she decided, and for that very reason her baiting of him seemed more enticingly dangerous. She could never be quite sure that Glenn wouldn't slap her down one of these days. Figuratively speaking, of course.

If he noted her quick scrutiny he gave no sign and Francie spoke softly in answer to his question: "I said I'd go."

"Oh, for gosh sakes!" He waited, breathing hard, before bursting out again. "Of all the low-down tricks. I ought to push you right out of this car and make you walk home, Francie Nelson."

She opened her eyes wide, looking at him with a pathos that might possibly have been real. She was very pretty in this dim light; her dark blue eyes seemed enormous, and her brown hair held shadows in its soft curls. Her expression was placatory, but Glenn would not understand it; he started the car and steered it with exaggerated caution between the deep splashing ruts of water until they came to the high road. Then he turned toward town, wordlessly.

"Where are you going?" asked Francie, whose soft tones might be concealing trepidation.

"I'm taking you home, right now."

She rather liked the reaction she was getting. They said nothing more as the car entered the outskirts of town. Francie pulled a vanity case out of her pocket and studied her face in the mirror, peering in snatches when they drove past the lamps of Main Street. Going by the jeweler's she noted the time was twelve-thirty. "Maybe Aunt Norah won't be sitting up," she commented in lightly ironic tones. "Oh, no!"

Glenn didn't reply, and she glanced at his profile. He looked firm-lipped and stony. She felt she had gone too far; suddenly she reached out and took his arm.

"Don't," said Glenn, keeping his eyes on the road. He shook off her hand.

"No, listen, Glenn. I was only kidding. I didn't tell him I'd go with him. I don't know who I'm going with yet, honestly. I just wanted to get a rise out of you."

"Well, you did, all right," said Glenn. He still sounded grim and unyielding. "Anyway, why don't you know yet who you're going with? Is it so hard to make up your mind as all that?"

"Yes," said Francie with a burst of honesty. "Frankly it is. I'm not even sure I'll go at all, if Aunt Norah goes on holding out about the dress. If I can't have that dress——"

"You never know what you want," said Glenn. "One of these days you'll find you can't pick and choose the way you're used to, and boy, wouldn't I like to be there to see it." Abruptly he braked the car at the side of the road, and turned and looked at her curiously.

"What are you thinking about?" she asked.

"I'm sort of summing you up," he said. "You're neat, all right. You don't need me to tell you that. But I can't figure out how you get to be such a nuisance. You're no better-looking than a lot of the others—even if you probably will be Beauty Queen, just because you're popular. Now Mary, for instance; Mary can run rings around you. And Gretta——"

"I know all about Gretta," said Francie tartly. "It's too cold to sit here having a row, Glenn. If you wouldn't mind taking me home now, so Aunt Norah won't worry——"

"In a minute, in a minute." The boy settled down, leaning on the wheel as if he had all the time in the world. His tone was cool and detached; it made Francie uneasy. "You're reasonably good-looking, yes, but not as good as all that. I don't know. I just don't see *why* you're the most popular girl in school."

"Well anyway, you admit I am. That's something." Indignation sharpened her voice. "If I'm so horrible, why do you bother me so much? That's what I can never understand."

"You're not horrible, exactly."

"Thanks for that much. Now please take me home."

"You're spoiled," said Glenn as if to himself. "Just spoiled. I don't know what it is; maybe we all let you get away with murder because you were always sort of romantic. Coming into Jefferson the way you did, your Mother dead and everybody remembering what a swell guy your Dad was, and so you seemed way ahead of the other girls even then—New York clothes and all that. I remember how you started out right away, doing exactly what you liked with us, wrapping us round your little finger. And we all let you. We still let you." He sat back, sighing, turned the key of the motor, and started the car again. Francie could think of nothing to say, which made her angrier than ever. "What's more, we'll go on the same way," he said. "I can see it. You'll get away with murder up at State too. Sometimes I wonder what your old man thinks about it all. If he lived here all the time, he'd see."

"Pop's satisfied, which evidently is a lot more than you are," said Francie.

"He doesn't know you like I do. He only sees you once in a while. Francie, it would do you all the good in the world to have the tar whaled out of you."

"Big he-man," she said mockingly. "Want to try it, Humphrey Bogart?"

"Me? Oh, no. Count me out. But some day you're going to be reformed. You'll meet somebody who won't let you walk all over him. Well——" They drew up before a pleasant-looking house set back in a green lawn. "I was going to say I want to be there when it happens, but I don't," said Glenn.

"Thanks for a wonderful time," said Francie. She took hold of the door-handle, and Glenn moved suddenly, pulling her towards him with his arm around her neck.

"Francie! I'm sorry I bawled you out," he muttered.

She was quiet. His kiss landed on the end of her nose. "Didn't you mean it all, then?" she asked.

"I—I don't know. I was so sore—— Come on, Francie, give me a kiss and say you'll go to Prom with me."

She pecked his cheek, and laughed, mollified. "I don't know about Prom, though. Let me go, Glenn; I've got to go, really. There's a light on; Aunt Norah's waiting up after all. Let go, Glenn, *please*."

"I'll see you tomorrow," he said.

Francie stood at the door before using her latchkey, trying to peer in through the frosted glass. Aunt Norah was not, after all, lurking there. But the hall light was on, and so was the lamp in the sitting room. She sighed more in boredom than in fear at the prospect of one of her aunt's gentle reprimands; with a defiant scratching of metal on metal she unlocked the door. She stopped short when she looked into the living room.

Aunt Norah wasn't there at all; a man sat alone at the desk in the sitting room, his back to the door, writing.

"Pop!" she cried in surprise. "When did you arrive?"

Fred Nelson put down his pen and swung around. He was a stocky man, gray-haired, with a firm, good-humored face and a confident, quiet manner. He spoke in deliberate tones, a deep, drawling voice. "Hello, Frances. Quite a night-bird, aren't you? I thought I'd give you just half an hour more to get home, before I turned in. How are you? Come over here under the light and let's see."

She kissed him and moved to a position under the light, where she turned in a slow circle like a fashion model, laughing.

"You look all right," he said at last, having inspected her solemnly. "Not as tired as I expected from what your aunt said."

"Why, what *did* she say?"

"Oh, just that you're kind of tearing around . . . I got here on the nine-twenty; I telegraphed this morning. Didn't you get my wire?"

"I guess it must have come all right, Pop, but I've been out since noon. I had a date. I do stay out a lot, these days."

"You look all right," he repeated.

As always when her father came to Jefferson, Francie was conscious of an embarrassed lag in the conversation. It was hard to talk to one's father when he didn't live at home. She had been ten when her mother died and she had moved to Jefferson to live with Aunt Norah. More and more after the change her father had been away, following his work in distant parts of the world. The arrangement had been successful as far as Francie's health and happiness were concerned. But when father and daughter were together again, they found themselves strangers, searching awkwardly for topics of mutual interest. Francie sensed this, but she didn't know what to do about it, and evidently Pop didn't either.

"Aunt Norah went to bed, did she?" she said at last.

"Yes, though I tried to make her wait. I wanted to talk to you in front of your aunt." Her father frowned slightly. "I particularly wanted a little family conference when you got in tonight, but she says she never knows when to expect you, and it's no use making plans. Now Francie, is that the truth? Do you mean to say you go cavorting all over the countryside at all hours of the night? If so, we'll have to have a change. I had no idea——"

"I don't know what you mean by cavorting," she retorted, flushing. "I don't go hanging around juke joints, if that's what it means. All the kids——"

"Now wait a minute, Frances, just wait a minute. I don't believe your little friends do act quite like this, with all this liberty, staying up until one o'clock on a week night, with school waiting in the morning."

"They're not 'little friends'," said Francie. "They're grown up. Like me."

"*Do* they stay up until all hours?" insisted her father.

"Some do. After all, Pop, I'm past seventeen. Most of the girls I know——"

He made an impatient gesture. "Oh, skip it. I really don't know how they run things nowadays, and I didn't mean to sidetrack myself. That isn't what I want to talk about. Sit down, honey, and let's be serious." Francie obeyed, somewhat apprehensively. He continued, "We've got to make a few plans, now you're graduating from high school. Did you have any sort of idea what you'd like to do next?"

Francie stared. "I thought that was all understood. I'm going up to State, aren't I? Like the rest of the crowd. We decided last time you were here, didn't we?"

"Yes, but things have changed a lot since then," said Mr. Nelson. He looked at the window, exactly as if the shade weren't down, she thought, as if he were looking at something outside. "I've given this matter a good deal of thought," he continued. "I had an idea sort of half-formed in my mind, and now the talk I've been having with your aunt has decided me. Francie, I've got to go back to Europe. For an indefinite period." He paused and waited for comment.

"Oh, really? I'm sorry, Pop. Or do you like the idea?"

"It's all right," said Fred Nelson. "I could have turned it down, but I didn't want to. They think things are going to open up in England in an important way . . . But you're not interested in all that, and why should you be? The point is, it affects you too."

"How?" asked Francie blankly. Never before had her father taken the trouble to talk very much of his affairs. He was always there in the background,

FRANCIE

kept away from Jefferson most of the year by his business, which was supremely uninteresting, as all adult businesses were to Francie and her friends. The other fathers would discuss these matters with Fred Nelson on his infrequent visits, but Francie never listened. She had never been expected to show any interest, and she simply accepted the world as she found it. It was an indulgent world, easy to live in. Her father supplied the money for her pretty clothes and all her little expenses; she had her allowance like the other girls, and never stopped to wonder seriously whether her father was well or badly off. She knew that the citizens of Jefferson, and even more important men in Chicago and New York respected his opinions and thought highly of him, but Glenn had given her a new glimpse of her parent tonight when he'd hinted that Fred Nelson contributed to her romantic background. Somehow she had liked to suppose that she was responsible for all the glamour herself, rather than having to give credit to a father who dropped in by plane now and then, to talk learnedly to the local businessmen about petroleum by-products.

"Are you going all over the world to sell petroleum?" she asked.

"I don't sell it, you little goose; I'm an executive. Did you think I carried it around in an oilcan?"

She giggled. "No, but honestly . . . where are you going, Pop?"

"England at first, maybe the Near East later.

We're expanding, following a plan we had under way before the war."

"Oh. Anything to do with politics? In Industrial History yesterday Miss Whitcombe said I ought to ask you more questions about things."

"Did she?" Pop looked surprised and pathetically gratified. "That was nice of her," he said, "but never mind all that just now. The point is, I'll be away from this part of the world for a long time. I don't know how you feel about this arrangement we've had with your Aunt Norah; probably you've never had any particular idea one way or the other. But I'm getting dissatisfied. I've been worrying about it. Among other considerations it appears to me I might as well not have a daughter at all, for all the good we get out of each other. Did you ever think of that?"

Francie reflected that there was something in what he said; she remembered having been jealous, in earlier years, because most of her friends had fathers to take them out on picnics during vacationtime, and she didn't; her father was always away. But she had got used to the situation long since. "It hasn't been so good," she admitted thoughtfully. "I thought it was the way you wanted it, though."

"I did want it for a while. There wasn't much else to do while you were a kid, now was there?" He stood up and walked across the room and back. She noticed for the hundredth time what a forceful person he seemed. "Francie, what would you say to leaving Jefferson?" he demanded suddenly.

"Leave Jefferson?" She was aghast. "Why, Pop, I couldn't right now. I just couldn't. I'm almost sure to be Beauty Queen this year. I mean, of course, I will leave when it's time to go to State, but if you mean right now——"

"I do mean right now, Francie." He looked sorry for her agitation, but determined anyway. "I've gone over and over it in my mind and this is the best way."

"You mean you want to take me with you to England?" she asked, as the horrid realization swept through her. Little as she knew her father in the everyday sense, she remembered of old how sudden and determined and unexpected he could be. She could recall one time when she'd been a little girl and Pop had made an abrupt decision about a vacation for all of them. It had been a trip her mother had not wanted to make, but once Pop had decided, there'd been no shaking him. He could be mild and indulgent and considerate for months on end, but when he really gripped a decision between his teeth, no one had ever been known to jar him free from it. Francie had a most unpleasant suspicion that this was going to be one of those times.

But it couldn't—it mustn't be!

"Pop, I *couldn't*," she said wildly. "You don't understand. I'm in my last term at school. The last term is *very important*. I'm going to be Beauty Queen, very likely, if Amy Muller isn't elected—and I don't think she will be. And I've got to go to Prom. And examinations, and college, and—Pop, you don't know what you're saying." She paused, panting. She could think of nothing but what she was threatened with losing.

"I do know. I know how hard it is, but I've decided it's best." That was his best bulldog manner. "You can make up your work in some school over there; I've asked the people at the office and they say you'll be way ahead of the others by the time we get back. The thing is, honey, I'll be in England close to a year. Possibly longer. You're growing up. Sooner or later we've got to get together; I want to see something of you before you run off and leave me; you'll be getting married before you know it. And you ought to see something of me, too. I know it's inconvenient——"

"Inconvenient!" In spite of the tears that were choking her, Francie laughed. He was knocking away the props of her whole life, and he called it inconvenient! "Pop, have you thought what I'll do with myself in a new place like England? I'll simply hate it." As she spoke she was convinced this was true.

"Well of course, if you make up your mind to hate it, that's that." Fred Nelson looked at her squarely, standing in the middle of the carpet, his hands shoved into his pockets. "But I wouldn't advise it, Francie. You go to bed and sleep on the idea; it's not so terrible as it sounds. Most girls would welcome the new experience, I should think. By the time you've been there a few months you'll be surprised; you'll——"

"I won't. I'll always hate it," she said, weeping.

"I can hardly blame you for feeling this way at first," said her father as if to himself. "You're used to a lot of attention, I understand. You queen it over the boys here in town. Well, all the better then to go away. Too much of that can't be good for you; you're an attractive girl if you *are* my daughter, but you need—— I'll tell you what it is, Francie; you're spoiled."

"Don't *you* give me that too," sniffled Francie into her handkerchief. "I've been listening to that all night." She scrambled to her feet, the handkerchief held to her nose. "I'm going to bed," she said. She ran out of the room, and her father watched her go, his face troubled but still determined.

CHAPTER 2

"IT DOES seem a shame." Francie's best friend, Ruth, spoke absently. The news had given her a good deal to think about. Plans needed rearranging, if the hub of her world was going to leave the scene.

Francie sat in the window seat of Ruth's bedroom, looking down into the front yard. The room was a pretty one, though perhaps a bit overfussy with its organdy bedspread and curtains to match. There were built-in wardrobes and a little ironing board that opened out, and the latest thing in indirect lighting, as Ruth's father was fond of electrical appliances. The girls were drinking chocolate malts which they had just mixed down in the kitchen. For a girl whose life was ruined, Francie was looking very cheerful; after thinking it over she had begun to feel excited at the widening prospect of life.

"I suppose you'll change your mind now about going to State? You'll have to," said Ruth.

"Pop said nearly a year. Maybe I can wangle it so as to get back home for State in the fall. Of course I may decide all over again not to go to college at all, though Pop blew his top over that last time I suggested it. Remember?"

"Yes, I do. What a row! Still, taking you away like this, he can hardly object if you don't want to come in later. That is, if you miss out on fall and have to come trailing behind the rest of us.

"I've given up Romance Languages, I think," Ruth went on. "I'm going in for psychology instead. More future to it. As for you, I'm beginning to think maybe you ought to go back to your original plan and be an artist."

This abrupt change of interest did not startle Francie; it was ordinary enough for the girls to make radical alterations in their life's ambition. They did it, on an average, weekly. Francie merely replied, "Oh well then, I think I'll do Political Science as a minor to Art. Pop says I'll have a good chance to look at practical Socialism; he says England's trying it out."

"Yes, there's that of course. But Francie, coming down to serious matters, it's terrible about Prom. And Beauty Queen. You were sure to get that. It's just the limit. Have you told Glenn about it?"

"I haven't told anybody, except you," said Francie. Her face grew doleful. "It is awful about Prom and all the rest. But Pop's got the bit between his teeth and there's not a bit of use making more fuss than I already have."

"You'll probably end by loving it. I know I'd give anything for the chance of a year abroad."

"Right now? I don't think you would," Francie said. "This is the most perfectly terrible time to be snatched out of school. The best years of our lives, or anyway months, and I'm going to miss them all. I'll never get over it . . . I wonder what English boys are like," she added.

"Cute, I should think. Listen, Francie, since you're not going to be here, what about Gretta for Glenn? I mean to say, she's really okay, she could be cute if she ever had a chance, and she hasn't got a date for Prom. I know it's tactless, talking like this as soon as you've told me about England, but you don't mind, do you?"

"Oh no, I don't mind." Francie went on studying the front yard, swinging her foot glumly. "I don't mind really," she added. "I get a boot out of the idea of adventure, to tell the truth. And there's one bright spot about the whole thing; even if Glenn does take Gretta to Prom and falls for her——"

"I don't mean he's likely to *fall* for her," interposed Ruth hastily. "It just seemed such a shame to waste him——"

"Even if he does, I don't care. I forgot to tell you, Pop's at least promised to give me a fur coat my next birthday if I get through the year without too much trouble. That's better than Prom, isn't it?"

"You are lucky, Francie. Of course it's better."

"Well, we'd better get downstairs to the phone and start in," said Francie with a sigh. "I'll have to call up everybody. Oh dear. And if you don't mind a word of advice, Ruth, I wouldn't go too fast on that Gretta proposition. Let Glenn think he thinks of it himself."

"You're telling me!" said Ruth. Laughing like young harpies, they went out of the room.

Fred Nelson put down the newspaper he had been trying to read for the last five minutes. He had no idea what was on the page. He said to his sister-in-law, peacefully knitting in her easy chair near the window, "Norah, what do you think about Francie?"

Aunt Norah took off her spectacles and blinked at him mildly. As she grew older she reminded him less and less of Francie's mother. But sometimes the trace of a smile that resembled her sister's crossed her face and he felt again the old pang of longing for someone lovely and gentle and lost. Francie was growing startlingly like her mother in appearance, though in a bolder, more spirited way.

"Think about Francie?" Aunt Norah repeated. "How can I think about her, Fred? She's too close. I try to keep her well-fed and happy, without interfering with her too much. Girls are so strong-willed these days."

"You must have some opinion. You can tell me at least if she worries you much." He pounced on her own phrase. "Strong-willed, you say? What do

FRANCIE

you mean by that? Is she one of these young girls who run away from home and are found a month later in Hollywood? Or is she likely to turn into one of these juvenile delinquents we hear so much about?"

"Dear me, Fred, what lurid notions you do get! Of course she won't do anything of the kind. She simply likes to have her own way, and I must say she usually manages to get it."

He tried another tack, since he was getting nowhere with his first one. "Tell me, Norah, do all young girls use as much lipstick as Francie? She has a nice mouth underneath all that junk, but you'd never know it."

"If you'll just look around you, you won't have to ask me," said Aunt Norah. "I can't make Francie behave any different from the others."

"And what goes on in her head?" continued Francie's father. "Judging from what I overhear on the telephone——"

"Oh, well," began Aunt Norah, polishing her spectacles agitatedly, "you can't go by that, completely."

"Boys, dates, and boys again," said Mr. Nelson. "Parties and boys, boys and parties. Gossip. Do they ever have a serious thought? She's not quite a child any more, Norah, but she doesn't seem to realize it."

"She's a good enough girl," said Aunt Norah. She put on her spectacles and began again to knit.

"She's not really grown up, you know. Let her enjoy life while she can."

"But what about school? Don't these young things ever do any homework?"

"No more than they must," admitted Francie's aunt, "but the school standards are high, and she keeps up. And she draws and paints a lot. She has her mother's talent for that. You'd be quite surprised if you knew how hard the child does work, sometimes. You wouldn't expect her to talk about *that* all the time to her friends, would you?"

"Well, maybe not." He was silent for a while, and then blurted, "The real trouble is that I'm worried, I guess. Francie's pretty."

"Oh yes, she's unusually pretty. Popular, too."

"Well. . . ." His voice trailed off.

"Too much of a responsibility, is that it?" asked Aunt Norah with a flash of shrewdness. "She's an American girl, Fred. American girls know how to take care of themselves anywhere."

"But *do* they? That's just it. Do they?"

"Frances will be all right, Fred. She's a normal, high-spirited American girl, and she's pretty as a picture, and you're going to be proud of her. You have to make allowances for occasional moods, considering the way you're uprooting her from her established rounds."

Still Mr. Nelson looked dubious. "Well, if you're not worried," he said, inconclusively. "Do you think you can get her ready in two weeks? Don't stint yourself on her clothes; I understand there's not much to buy nowadays, over there."

Francie had looked forward to being wretchedly unhappy all the time, or at least for a while every day, before they sailed, but somehow she never found the time. There was the prospect of farewell parties, with lots of the boys protesting they would miss her too much to enjoy themselves, at least for weeks; there was shopping; there was the prospect of several days in New York, with more shopping. She had to help Aunt Norah pack her glass and china for storage. Aunt Norah was intending to sublet the house and spend some months in Florida, now that she need not make a home for her niece.

"One good thing about all this," Francie confided to her aunt as she wrapped silver fish-knives in flannel, "is that I'm finding out at last who are really my friends and who aren't. Some of the girls are being awfully catty—their names would surprise you."

"You'll forget all these little pinpricks by the time you're across the Atlantic," said Aunt Norah cheerfully. "I must say it makes me marvel, the way young people change from generation to generation. To look at you, anybody would think you'd been condemned to a prison cell, instead of getting a real treat. What wouldn't I have given for your chance at your age!"

"Yes, Aunt Norah, but times aren't at all the same any more. I know people used to want more than anything to go to Europe. We had to read Henry James and all those for English. But don't forget, it's different nowadays. It's the War that did it. You just talk to some of the G.I.'s and you'll find out. I'd never have a better time anywhere else than here, honestly. I know that."

"You know everything, of course," sighed Francie's aunt. "It's not a bit of use my arguing. Well, I must say it's nice to think you like your own home so much."

"Not that I want to be narrow-minded," added Francie judiciously. "It's just that the time is inconvenient, but I'm perfectly willing to give England a *chance*."

It was decided in Francie's crowd that her going-away should be marked, if not exactly celebrated, by a series of social gatherings. Movies, they felt, were not enough; everyone went to the movies whenever there was a new picture anyway. A dance in the high-school gym had already been scheduled for the week before and the crowd couldn't very well hold another one so soon again, just before the going-away day. Instead, a party at someone's house was indicated. But whose? Glenn, Ruth and Gretta, meeting at the Chocolate Shoppe by chance, argued about it.

"Let *me* have it," begged Gretta. "It's my turn really, and I'd love to give Francie a going-away party." Gretta was the doll-pretty type and everybody knew that if it wasn't for Francie she might go all out for Glenn.

"I know you would," said Ruth with heavy meaning in her tone, "but after all I'm her closest friend and I do think——"

"We could throw a good one at our place," said Glenn, "if we give Mother enough notice."

They had not settled the question by the time Francie appeared for her morning snack, and they turned to her for decision.

"Oh, it's got to be at our own house," she said immediately. "Aunt Norah would be terribly hurt, you know she would, if I went anywhere else on my last night. It's nice of you all and I *do* appreciate it, but. . . ." Her voice grew tremulous; she broke off. The tactful Ruth changed the subject. They all gave in to the overpowering argument of Aunt Norah's feelings, and Francie won the day.

"They couldn't have argued," said Francie, reporting on the arrangement when she went home for lunch. "I just told them that would be the way you wanted it, Aunt Norah."

"That was right, Francie," Fred Nelson approved. He looked gratified at Aunt Norah's pleasure, and later when Francie had left the room he said to her, "She's not so self-centered as I was afraid she might be. That showed real sensibility."

"Oh, Francie's got the right instincts," said Aunt Norah indulgently. "Francie and I understand each other."

"It will be fun to see a kid's party again," said Pop, musing aloud. "I haven't seen one since I was a kid myself. I begin more and more to realize I've missed a good deal, one way and another, working so hard while Francie was growing up."

Aunt Norah looked at him, opened her mouth, but then thought better of whatever she had been going to say.

The important last evening arrived finally. Pop sat in the living room, looking around with a tolerant smile at the preparations. Aunt Norah was in the kitchen in her good silk print with an apron over it, putting out glasses and depositing Coca-cola and ginger-ale bottles in the icebox, which had been cleared for the purpose. The doors between the dining room and living room were open; the dining-room table had been shoved back into a corner and the carpet was rolled up. The first guest's step was heard on the porch and a young girl walked into the hall without ringing.

"Hi!" she called up the stairs. "Francie? I'm here!"

When she saw Pop she hesitated a moment, then came forward to shake hands, rather shyly. Francie ran down the steps. A boy with a crew cut arrived; the party was under way. The young people perched on chair arms, curled up on sofas, or slumped almost on the backs of their necks in chairs. No one, Pop observed, seemed to use furniture in the more conventional manner to which he was accustomed.

They soon were talking animatedly about their

own mysterious affairs, in a language Pop could not understand. Feeling very much out of it, he sought Aunt Norah in the kitchen.

"Are the children getting on all right?" she asked, taking off her apron and hanging it up on the door.

"Very well indeed. Very well. Fine-looking lot of youngsters," said Pop. "Not that I can tell one from another, except Francie and little what's-her-name —Ruth. And Glenn, naturally. I'd know Glenn by this time, even if he didn't have all those freckles, he's been around so much."

Aunt Norah said, "Well, if they're started off, I don't know that we've got any more duties to perform out here. Let's go."

"Go? Why, where are we going?"

"Out," said Aunt Norah.

"Why? Where?"

"As for why," said Aunt Norah hesitantly, "that's rather hard to answer. Francie likes to have the old folks out when she has a party, so I always leave them to themselves."

Fred Nelson began, angrily, "Well, if that isn't the most outrageous——" but Aunt Norah's gentle voice continued.

"As for where, it's for you to decide if you'd rather just drive around somewhere—or we could see the new picture at the Odeon, or go and call on the Tuckers. I know they're at home because I asked when I met Mrs. Tucker at the Stop and Shop."

Pop stood squarely in front of his sister-in-law, so that she was forced to look at him. "Listen to me, Norah," he said. "You know it's all wrong, as well as I do, to leave those children in charge of the house. It's—it's unheard-of! It's unmannerly of them to expect it! Our mothers would turn in their graves if they knew. What's come over this country? What's the matter with all the parents to permit this sort of thing? Have they gone crazy, or what?"

"Why shouldn't the youngsters be left, Fred? Don't you trust them?"

He made an impatient gesture. "That's not the point—that's not at all the point. It's the *manners* aspect that makes me sore. It's your house. Why should you be dispossessed of your house simply because a lot of selfish kids want to get together and have a party?"

"Oh Fred!" She laughed helplessly. "What a queer way to look at it! It's easy to see you haven't kept up. Children have it their own way nowadays. As for me, I don't see why not."

"Why not? Why not? Do you mean to say you don't resent being kicked out to wander around all the evening because these young cubs haven't the manners——"

"If I'm not wanted here," said Aunt Norah, "I don't want to *be* here. Now you just calm down a minute, Fred, and be reasonable. Of course we could perfectly well insist on staying here, and attend the party, and spoil their fun. If you insist on it, that's what we'll do. But it's Francie's last night and——"

"But why should it spoil their fun if we did? What's the matter with you all? Why can't we all get along together, even if we *are* different ages?"

"Now that's a question," said Aunt Norah, "that's too big for any one woman to answer. You can't fight Nature, and young people like to stick to their own kind. Do you want to embarrass poor Francie on her last night, and spoil her party, perhaps drive all her friends out somewhere else where they can feel they aren't being watched? They weren't brought up as we were, remember, with chaperones watching us every minute, and all that."

"Why, no, I——"

"Do you really think you ought to go in and sit down there, and try to talk to a lot of kids who have nothing to say to you?"

"Of course not! It's just that the system's all wrong," said Pop, "but I'm just as glad I'm getting Francie out of this for a little while. Maybe in another sort of civilization she'll realize that parents have some rights too!"

Aunt Norah shook her head and sighed.

"Well, come on. If we've got to go, we've got to go," said Pop, "unless we feel we ought to go upstairs instead and skulk in our own rooms. I guess the other way *is* less awkward. I suppose that's why you long-suffering older generation evolved it."

He looked in at the party as he and Aunt Norah paused, coated and hatted, on their way to the front door. With difficulty he refrained from glowering. A few couples—Francie was among them—were dancing to the radio which was turned up to deafening volume. Others were in groups, animatedly discussing things which Pop either did not understand or thought they did not understand, and doing it at the top of their lungs to be heard above the music. He noticed several couples holding hands not at all self-consciously.

"We're off, children," called Aunt Norah.

Francie waved, hesitated, and then on a sudden warm impulse ran over to kiss them both. She looked flushed, happy, and very pretty. Out on the front porch, Pop blew his nose. "She's not so bad," he said. "Spoiled—all of them are spoiled—but she's a nice kid."

"I'm glad you're beginning to realize that!" said Aunt Norah.

"Well, come on then," Pop said, as he led the way to the car. "If we're to go into exile for the whole evening, let's get going!"

Time flew by faster than Francie had ever known it to go. Before she could catch her breath, before she had really accepted this uprooting deep down inside her, the parting time had come and she and Pop were on the train rushing east.

However dizzy and breathless she felt, she found New York absolutely heavenly. She was in a hurry to write Ruth about it, and yet in a hurry to do more running around outside the hotel: two theaters in one day, the stores, "21" and the Stork

Club for lunch with Pop, the stores again, the Metropolitan Museum and the Museum of Modern Art, which nearly knocked the stores out of her mind and made her dig her sketchbook out of the bottom of her suitcase; then a hairdresser's and again the stores.

Two whole hours one afternoon she spent wandering the plazas and corridors of Radio City, trying to satisfy her urge to capture these crowded impressions in sketches on paper. Her rough drawings did not please her, but Pop seemed astonished and impressed.

"That's a big chunk of talent you have, Francie. You're better than your mother already, and she was pretty good."

She found herself thinking often of her mother in New York. She knew her mother had loved the city, and Francie, feeling closer to her than she had for a long while, loved it too.

"I'm nearly dead," she wrote at last, in a quiet space forced on her by the time of day, when nothing was open for shopping. "Oh Ruth, I've had the most divine time with the paintings. There are lots to be seen in small galleries, I just found out, and I'm so excited I can hardly wait to get back to work. I've done some sketching here, of course, but I mean seriously back to work. I wonder sometimes if it wouldn't be a complete waste of time, going to State. Art is after all my only *true* interest." She added another line under "true" and paused, nibbling at her pen, to look into the hotel mirror. It was a pity she hadn't waited to buy all her sweaters and things here, she mused. They had a better look, somehow. If Ruth could only see the yellow twin set she had on right now. . . .

". . . my only *true* interest. . . ." She smiled at the words. Her head was such a tumble of interests at the moment.

"Pop has given me my head in the way of last-minute clothes and I've gone mad, so it's just as well you and I decided against that blue tweed coat. I did much better here at Saks'. Pop's being absolutely sweet about everything, and sometimes I think I've never done him justice. He isn't just a businessman at all, though he seems to be pretty good at that by the way—it might sound like boasting if I told you how they treat him at his office. But he isn't as difficult as I've always thought. For one thing, he didn't mind my getting a hair-do at Antoine's. Also, anybody less understanding would probably make me trail along to Central Park Zoo. Of course, I wasn't above doing some of the touristy things, like Radio City and going to the top of the Empire State Building, and I loved that—but I kept thinking of Doris the time her father showed her around New York and treated her like a baby. Pop at least lets me pick out my own clothes, and he orders my meals as if I were grown up. (I wouldn't know what to pick, anyway.) I'm waiting in the hotel room now because he had to go to the office to wind up a lot of things, but I'll phone down soon for a coke and start dressing. Tonight we're going to the theater again, and tomorrow we actually *sail*. I'm feeling much better about England and everything. If Pop's going to be as decent as this all the time I haven't got a thing to worry about."

While Francie was scribbling away so happily, Fred Nelson at his desk in the office sorted out a few last papers and chatted to his secretary. "I'm afraid I've neglected things this trip, Miss Peterson," he said, "but I've got my little girl with me, and you know how it is."

"Don't I, Mr. Nelson. There's nothing like the responsibility of a child in a big city."

"Francie's not a child any more," said Mr. Nelson, sighing. "I only wish she were. She's so sure she's grown up. . . ."

"It must be a great problem," said Miss Peterson.

"Well, I'm letting her have her head just these few days. It's going to be a big change for her over there. Of course I've been doing the Near and Far East and haven't been in England since before the war. But we hear enough about it. I'm afraid she won't have the sort of fun she's accustomed to. So I'm being indulgent."

"Don't you worry, Mr. Nelson; she'll land on her feet all right after a little while. It's only that life in England is apt to be drab just now, isn't it? I get letters from the girl in our office over there, so I know something about it. You tell your little girl to buy plenty of warm underthings. And take candy along, and butter; that's what my girl friend tells me."

"Butter?" Fred Nelson looked horrified, as only a hotel-dweller can be horrified at such a domestic suggestion.

"Oh yes. It comes in cans, you know. Of course you can leave a standing order here for those things. I'd better wait until you find out for yourself," said Miss Peterson.

"Well then, I guess I'll run along." Mr. Nelson picked up his hat from the desk. "That just about winds it up, I think. I promised Francie I'd take her somewhere nice and lively for dinner before the show."

"That's right. Give her a good time the last night, poor kid," Miss Peterson said, and it was probably just as well that Francie could not hear her sympathetic words.

CHAPTER 3

It was a cold, raw day. The tossing sea was lead-colored. Francie sat in her deck chair, wrapped in a ship's blanket, luxuriating in gloom. It had been a rough trip. Her father was seasick, the other people who ate at their table were seasick, and Francie was beginning to wonder if she herself were altogether well. Perhaps not, she thought. She had waked up that morning with the urge to paint. Not just sketch, as she had in New York, but to try something more ambitious. Today, she resolved, she would paint a picture with the sea in it, that sea which had so excited her when she first saw it in New York. But when she got up and dressed and made her way down the slanting, tipsy corridor to knock on the door of her father's cabin, discomfort caused her to forget about painting. She wanted only to get out on deck and breathe fresh air.

Now, comfortable again and looking down a

vista of empty deck chairs, she began to feel proud. "It really must be rough," she thought. "Practically everybody's laid up. I must be tougher than I thought."

At the end of the line of chairs, next to the place where the deck narrowed, she saw a girl of her own age whom she had noticed the day before, sitting as she herself was sitting, wrapped in a blanket. She was a pretty, fair-haired girl, dressed very much like Francie, though Francie took that for granted. In Jefferson the girls chose their clothes from local stores, and meekly followed the styles *en masse*.

"I wonder," thought Francie, "if she's nearly sick too?"

The girl probably felt someone looking at her, because she turned her head and met Francie's gaze. She smiled. "Are you a good sailor?" she said across the chairs.

"I was just wondering," said Francie dubiously. "How do *you* feel?"

The girl laughed a little. "I don't want to ask myself," she said. "Maybe we ought to take a walk; shall we?"

They made their way down to the end of the deck and around the windy side, where it was impossible to shout above the gale. By the time they had done the round once they felt like old friends.

"Your first trip?" asked Francie.

"No, I've crossed once, the other way. In '41."

"Once?"

"I'm English," explained the girl.

"You don't talk a bit like an English person."

"I've been in the States all this time. I'm practically American by this time. I'm Penelope Harley."

"I'm Francie Nelson . . . Are you going home now?"

"Yes. I came over as an evacuee, it seems so long ago now. It seems forever." She looked pensive, and Francie gazed admiringly at her. The new girl was slender, with a confident sort of style in the way she wore her clothes.

"Are your parents with you?" Francie asked at last, when they had been duly buffeted on the windward side, and were back again in shelter.

"My people? No, they didn't come with me, you know. It was Mummy who said I must come to America. I wasn't very keen on it and Daddy was absolutely against it from the very beginning. He was Navy; he didn't like the idea of sending off his child if all the other children in England couldn't be shipped to safety at the same time."

"What a funny idea," said Francie.

Penelope looked at her. "Do you think so? I don't, especially; I understood the way he felt. I held out, too, for a long time, until all the other children who were going had already gone. But Mummy couldn't bear it. As soon as she was left alone, I was sent." Penelope talked as if to herself, arguing with someone in memory. "I tried not to go even then, but the suspense was too much for

FRANCIE

her, I suppose . . . She was only thinking of my good."

"I hope you went to nice people," said Francie. She did understand the "funny idea" after all, she realized. She had a bad habit of calling anything new funny and pushing it away, she reflected.

"Oh, they weren't strangers. It wasn't as bad as that. I went to cousins, and they couldn't have been nicer. It was fortunate after all that Mummy was so stubborn, the way things turned out. I'm not boring you, I hope?"

"No, no. Do please go on." Francie gripped her new friend's arm as they plunged again into the wind. She had long ago forgotten that she wasn't feeling well.

"Daddy was killed," said Penelope.

"Oh, how awful."

"Mine sweeping," said Penelope. "Most of the men in his ship were lost with him. When my aunt heard the news she begged Mummy to come over as well, to be with us, and Mummy wouldn't."

"Why wouldn't she?" asked Francie.

"Oh, she—she just had to stand by after his death. Do her part, you know."

"Yes, I see what you mean. But how awful for you."

Penelope didn't reply. In a companionable silence they continued around and around.

"You've had a romantic sort of life," Francie said at last. "It makes me feel very ordinary."

43

"Why ordinary? Is this your first time across the Atlantic?"

"Yes. I haven't really been anywhere in the world but the Middle West," Francie explained. With a novel sense of humility she took her turn and told the story of her life. It seemed, all of a sudden, rather prosy; she forgot she was Jefferson's glamour girl. "So now I'm going abroad for the first time," she said.

Penelope said, "You couldn't feel any more afraid of a new country than I do of my own. It's quite as if I were immigrating; I've forgotten all I ever knew about England."

"Why didn't you go back sooner? After all, the war's been over quite a while."

Penelope looked uncomfortable, but before Francie could retract her careless question, the English girl went on.

"There were—difficulties. At first Mummy was working and there wasn't any place for me. And then—well, she married again and it seemed wiser somehow for her to get used to her new life before I came over. Not that she didn't want me. . . ."

She broke off, her fair skin flushing painfully, and Francie hurried to ask a safer question. "Are you going on with school, or have you decided to quit?"

"Oh, I'm going on, for one more year at any rate. I want to stay away from home until I can see how things are."

"Away from home?" repeated Francie, puzzled. "Oh, you mean you're going to *boarding* school, of course. Pop told me but I forgot for a minute; there are lots of boarding schools in England, aren't there? At home not everybody goes away, but you probably know that."

"I do know. I ought to; I went to day school myself in New Hampshire. But boarding school is what one does in England, and I must say it's going to be convenient for me, since Mummy's married again, and I don't know my stepfather. Maybe I won't like him, and he's sure to be wondering about me too, if we'll get on and all that. Well, of course we'll get on; I mean, we've got to. But if it's an effort, I'm better away at school, don't you think? Where I can figure out what my next move should be."

"Oh yes, Penelope. How hard it must be." The ship or the rough weather or some other unusual circumstance gave Francie a new impulse toward friendship. She felt drawn toward this girl whom she had found for herself.

The wind died down slowly. Forgetful of the weather the two girls lounged in deck chairs and chattered until the moment when the deck stewards came around with cups of beef tea. Afterwards they went to play table tennis.

Francie managed to do some painting after all when the weather grew calmer, and she found in Penelope not the worshiping admiration she had

had from Ruth back home, but a more understanding and critical eye. Penelope really understood that a girl might have a yearning to do something big with a talent because she herself burned with high ambition. The English girl was interested in the theater. Not in the acting end, but in stage-managing and producing. Her school in New Hampshire had given her some opportunity to develop her talents and she hoped eventually to do something with them professionally.

"Though I haven't told Mummy about this yet," she confessed to Francie. "I'm not sure she won't be frightened by the mere mention of the theater. And of course I've no idea how Uncle Jim will react. It's better, I think, to let them in gradually on how I feel."

Francie noted that concern about Uncle Jim, her stepfather, and how he would react about this and that, punctuated most of Penelope's talk. She was glad that no such anxiety faced her as beset her new friend.

What with painting and talking, walking and deck games, the crossing was over before they knew it, and it was morning of the last day. The ship was moving slowly into dock at Southampton when Francie came out to watch. She had got up early, but she found Penelope there before her, standing very still on the deck, her hands shoved deep into her coat pockets. Her yellow hair blew in the wind, but she didn't try to smooth it, and she didn't notice Francie coming toward her at the rail. She was deep in thought and she looked rather apprehensive, staring ahead at England.

Francie cleared her throat, and Penelope jumped.

"Oh, there you are. All packed and ready?"

"Packed, but not exactly ready. What do you suppose we do now?" said Francie. Should she say something encouraging? Perhaps Penelope wouldn't like being understood; better not.

"I suppose it's good-bye for the time being," said Penelope. "Your father says you're going straight on to London and he'll decide your fate after that, but my people live in the New Forest, and I expect they'll be on the dock now, waiting for me. It's only a short drive away as Americans count distance. But we must keep in touch." She was quite gay now.

"Yes, we will. Anyway I will," said Francie, "though I guess you'll be awfully busy picking up where you left off. By the way, Penny, Pop says he'd like to know more about whatever school you go to."

"Fairfields? I'll give him the address and he can telephone the headmistress if he likes. Or wait, Mummy might know more about it than he's likely to hear from one of the staff. He'd better phone Mummy. Later he can ask the school secretary to send him a prospectus."

"That would be fine," said Francie without enthusiasm. The prospect of an English school did not intrigue her, though she wanted to keep in touch with Penelope.

"It may be full up, but sometimes there are last-minute cancellations. Usually, in fact. . . ." Penelope turned from the rail. "There's the breakfast gong—our last meal before we dive into the land of austerity. I hope you remember that, Francie, and eat hearty. I'll be seeing you later at the customs shed."

She smiled and waved, but Francie could see that she was agitated, nevertheless. And no wonder, she mused, with all these new adjustments she must begin to make as soon as the ship docked.

Francie sighed, remembering that she had a few adjustments to worry about on her own account. She wondered anxiously if she were properly dresssed. When asked, Penny had suggested country-type clothes for traveling, and sensible shoes. People in England didn't try to look smart for the train, Penny said.

Francie went down to the salon for breakfast. All around her she heard travelers making the same joking remarks about austerity, and talking about how much they were going to eat for the last meal: eggs, and waffles, and plenty of butter and sugar. She found Pop at their table, already halfway through his breakfast.

"Sit down, honey, and be sure you eat enough," he said. "Your last chance, remember."

FRANCIE

Francie sat down opposite him and stared at the menu without reading it. "I don't think I could eat a thing," she said.

It was all a queer mixture. Francie found she couldn't put it down neatly arranged in a descriptive letter, though she had promised Ruth and Glenn to tell them every single thing she thought about England as soon as she'd looked it over. How could one describe the jumble England was? Many things were exactly like what she'd expected, but they didn't separate themselves from the rest. A modern tobacco store was housed in an eighteenth-century bow-windowed cottage, right bang in the middle of a wide thoroughfare in the middle of London. An old woman wearing a peasant's broad-brimmed sort of hat sold flowers at the door of the American-looking department store called Selfridge's. Francie was always being reminded of movies or plays she had seen about England's history, and of Dickens' books where there were lots of illustrations, but between these moments there were other glimpses of an ugly industrial country she'd never expected to find.

The first time she saw a policeman in a helmet she clapped her hands and cried to Pop, "Look, just like the pictures!" A moment later their taxi swept them into the district of Camden Town where they rode past long dreary streets of depressing sooty little houses all joined together. "Is *this*

London?" she demanded in disgust and disappointment. "Oh, it's horrid. So dull!"

"No worse than some of our slums, in fact not as bad, but you've just not bothered to look around in New York," said Pop. "Now then, it's not so bad, is it?"

Looking at the terraces at Regent's Park, Francie was appeased. Those gracious curves and crescents and the lake winding through the Park were better than any pictures or movies. Suddenly they came to a great gap in the buildings, where a bomb had done terrific damage. Half-destroyed walls and smoke-blackened empty window frames marred the lovely picture.

"It will be a long time before they can rebuild that," said Pop, shaking his head. Francie was too appalled to speak.

Before Pop dived into his work he spared a few days to go sightseeing with his daughter. They visited St. Paul's and Kew Gardens, and found their way to Rye.

"You'd think we were living in some other century," said Francie as they walked down a twisting, hilly, cobbled street between black-and-white cottages. "Queer, to think people just go on living in these museum pieces."

The weather behaved itself during the first days, but one morning they found the street swirling with thick white mist, and Francie thought it might be the famous London fog. "No," said Pop, "this isn't a real old-fashioned pea-souper. I was just asking the clerk. He says you don't get many of those any more, where you can't see where to put your foot next. Once in a while it happens, but not so much. This damp gets into your bones, doesn't it, chicken?"

Walking with Pop down Bond Street, Francie agreed absently, and turned to stare after two women who had just passed them in that famous district where everyone was supposed to be smartly dressed. The women, she reflected, looked simply weird in their old-fashioned tweed coats and their hats like Boy Scout headgear, trimmed with birds' wings. Yet they seemed quite satisfied with themselves. They were obviously confident they looked nice. "I wonder what it feels like," thought Francie for the first time, "not to be an American."

The fleeting wonder came back to her now and again. She marveled when she saw crowds gathered at the gates of Buckingham Palace, patiently standing for hours, hoping for a glimpse of some member of the royal family. The Palace itself seemed imposing enough; it resembled a great central public library. But the simple, eager curiosity of the people puzzled her. "I'd like to see them myself," she thought, "but not enough to wait all those hours."

And life in England was so quiet! She was told that the streets had been busier before petrol was rationed, and before the lights had to be dimmed at night to save coal. But it wasn't only that, she knew. The strange stubby taxis weren't fitted out with radios, that was one thing; music didn't blare out as she walked past shop doorways. Even the hotel lounge had no radio or other musical device.

One afternoon Francie, left alone, went into a moving-picture house in Oxford Street. The picture was one she had seen in Jefferson, but then it had not had much effect on her. Now, the sound of American speech and a familiar tune sent a wave of nostalgia over her and she nearly wept. After a little, however, she forgot where she was. Everything in the picture seemed natural, and when she stepped out into the dim quiet underlit street afterwards it was as if she had herself walked off the screen, suddenly coming from a normal world into this.

"A lady asking for you," said the desk clerk on the telephone. "Mrs. Tennison."

"Oh yes." Francie was doubtful, but she didn't want him to know she was not sure she had understood him correctly. The English accent *was* difficult. "A lady, did you say? Waiting for me?"

"Yes, miss."

"Tell her I'll be right down, will you?"

"I beg your pardon, miss?" Evidently the clerk had just as much trouble understanding Francie as Francie had understanding the clerk.

"I'm—coming—down—now."

"Oh, right you are. Coming now, madam," she heard over the telephone before she hung up.

Let's see now, she thought. Mrs. Tennison—that would be the lady Pop had spoken of as his British associate's wife. Pop had said at breakfast, "I'll have to leave you on your own today, Francie, but Mrs. Tennison seems to be a nice woman. She's very kindly asked me if she couldn't give me a hand and show you around while Bob and I are going over the general picture, and I said I was sure you'd be tickled to death."

"I would like it," said Francie. "It would be nice to have a native guide." Pop raised his eyebrows and she grinned at him. "Well—you know what I mean. I get tired of just going around looking in windows, and I feel shy, too. It isn't as if I could buy anything. Why, I tried to buy some candy yesterday. The man had it all wrapped up, and then I found out I needed candy coupons or something, only he said 'sweet' coupons. Was my face red!"

"But honey, why didn't you buy candy if you wanted? You could have. You've got all your coupons," said Pop. "I gave you the book yesterday morning."

"Was that what you gave me? How was I to know? I had it in my bag the whole time."

"I told you," said Pop, giving his daughter an impatient look. "You're just dreaming half the time and don't listen. It's a sort of laziness . . . Well, you just ask Mrs. Tennison about all that. She said she'd come around about eleven."

Now, Francie hurried to put on her hat, and

paused for a last look in the rather bad mirror, in the definitely bad light. She had her coat on already. She always wore her coat. She complained each morning to her father that a coat was a regular part of indoor clothing in this country: even when she had it on she didn't feel warm. Fred Nelson always said, "You'd better get some regular long underwear, then," and Francie retorted that she'd *die* before she wore long underwear. Today she wondered if she really would prefer death!

Her lipstick needed repair, she noted; she carefully applied more, and surveyed the result. There, that was all right. She straightened the seams of her nylons, pulled on beige capeskin gloves and stepped out of the room to the elevator.

She rang the bell and waited, looking around with simple, fresh curiosity at the corridor, all upholstered in dusty heavy dark red plush and velvet. The English interiors she'd seen were all awfully dark, she reflected. In America, especially if they had so many cloudy days, the houses would be painted and decorated in bright light colors which would give a sunny effect. Nobody in Jefferson went in for dark red curtains or carpets. And the brown colors one saw here; the depressing paneled walls, the——

Francie realized suddenly that the elevator wasn't showing any signs of life. She rang again, peremptorily. Another long wait produced nothing, not so much as a twitching rope, so at last she decided

FRANCIE

to walk down the staircase she saw at the end of the hall, spaciously carpeted and very gloomy.

Downstairs near the information desk a lady stood waiting. She was solid-looking, dressed in a sensible, rather bunchy green tweed suit and a brown felt hat that would have been much better if it had not been trimmed with a big green velvet flower. Francie observed these details absently, because she always summed up feminine costumes instinctively; but it didn't occur to her for a moment or two that the lady might be her Mrs. Tennison. The lady didn't think of the connection either. She looked at Francie and then glanced toward the stationary, empty elevator with the shabby stool that stood beside it. The elevator man was apparently off duty. At last the clerk behind the desk saw Francie, recognized her as she stood looking around, and said something to the lady in tweeds. The lady raised her eyebrows and walked over purposefully.

"Miss Nelson?"

"I'm Miss Nelson . . . Oh, are *you* Mrs. Tennison?"

They shook hands. "But I was expecting a little girl, not a young woman," said Mrs. Tennison in a nice full voice. "Sorry to have been so stupid. I understood——"

"Did Pop tell you I was a little girl?" Francie was indignant.

"No, he didn't. He told me your age, that's all."

As she spoke Mrs. Tennison glanced at Francie's clothes, her stockings, her carefully made-up mouth. "I suppose I've forgotten what pretty clothes look like," she said soothingly. "You mustn't mind me; I'm hopelessly provincial. We all are nowadays, you know. Now you must tell me, Frances, what you'd like to do. This isn't the best time in history to visit London, but we'll do what we can for you. I had thought of a visit to the Park before we have luncheon—Stewart's is most convenient for that, I always think—and then perhaps we might do the Tower or Madame Tussaud's. It's for you to say; perhaps you'd prefer to look around the shops?"

Francie hesitated. She wasn't daunted by the necessity of making a choice; it was only that she couldn't recognize what sort of amusement she was being offered.

"Such a pity my little girl Jennifer isn't here to help us out," continued Mrs. Tennison kindly, "but she's at school until the end of term, of course. *She'd* put me right in no time. *She'd* know what you would like."

Francie had a sudden vision of a child in a short dress, piloting her by hand through the confusing wrong-way traffic. She nearly giggled aloud.

"But you'll have to meet her as soon as ever she gets back," Mrs. Tennison was saying as she led the way through the front door and into the street. "In the meantime—have you any idea at all of what you'd care to do on your first outing? No doubt you've already looked around a bit for yourself?"

Francie confessed that she had been afraid of going too far afield. "I've just walked around near the hotel when Pop wasn't with me, and looked in store windows. You know how it is."

Mrs. Tennison laughed a little and said, "We'll take the bus to Westminster Abbey, then, and look at the Houses of Parliament from outside and after that we can decide about lunch. Most Americans seem to enjoy looking at the Abbey, and I'd rather like to see it again myself. One never does go, somehow."

Meekly Francie trotted after her guide, who strode along in flat-heeled shoes at a pace which left the American girl breathless. A tall narrow red bus swooped toward them in the narrow street. Francie started straight for the door, but Mrs. Tennison held her back.

"We must take our places in the queue, my dear," she said, and led her charge to the rear of a line of would-be bus-riders who stood quietly on the pavement, stepping up one by one in a manner strangely polite.

"Move along, please. Move along, please," the conductor kept saying in a courteous voice, and the people did move along. Francie stared at their calm faces. She nearly told Mrs. Tennison how different it all was from home, but at the thought of describing it—the rushing people in American streets, the happy-go-lucky, furious, catch-as-catch-can of the crowds getting into buses or onto trains, the cheerful insults exchanged between bus-drivers and taxi-drivers—she remained silent. It would have been impossible. These people were a different race, she told herself. She sat quietly at Mrs. Tennison's side, shivering in the damp dank air, and felt miserably out of place, violently homesick.

CHAPTER 4

"Aren't you feeling well?" asked Pop. He couldn't see Francie very clearly. Though every light in the dining room was lit, the lamps hung very high over the tables, most of which were empty. A dispirited, spectacled waitress lingered near the door, obviously wishing the Nelsons would finish their dinner and go away.

"I feel all right," said Francie, surprised. "Why shouldn't I?"

"Maybe you're tired from your day out, but you sound unusually quiet to me."

"Tired?" Francie opened her eyes wide and began to laugh. She took a small bite of boiled potato. "Why would I be tired? Mrs. Tennison and I just went to see that Abbey, and after lunch to the Zoo. I'll tell you what's the matter, Pop; Mrs. Tennison made me nervous and I was thinking about that, I guess. She treats me like—I don't know how to describe it. She's very slow and patient and kind, and talks to me carefully, as if I were a dumbbell or an immigrant."

"Well, you are an immigrant, in a way," said Fred Nelson.

"Yes, but I'm not a baby immigrant, and I'm not half-witted. Though before lunch was finished I began to wonder about that. Honestly, I did try to be good. I tried not to be dreamy, the way you and Aunt Norah get so mad at."

"Was she rude? I can't imagine Bob Tennison's wife——"

"No, no, Pop, nothing like that. She was terribly kind. Only she obviously thought I was, well, a minor. She has ideas about young girls. Young girls are children, she thinks. She thinks my clothes are all wrong. No, of course she didn't say so, but she does. She's tactful, but she underrates my intelligence. I knew what she was thinking." Francie paused, somewhat abashed by her long speech, but her father wasn't reacting as she feared he would. He only looked thoughtful.

"There'll be a good deal of that kind of thing, I guess. You'll have to get used to it," he said. "Something of the sort happens to me too."

This was a new idea, that the all-conquering Pop might ever feel inadequate. Francie's heart warmed to him. She wanted to offer reassurance.

"She's awfully nice, really, Pop; she took the whole day off just to help me out, and that was very kind. Oh, by the way, it's a funny coincidence; you know Penelope?"

"Penelope? Oh yes, the girl on the boat. Nice girl."

"Well, Penny's going back to her old school for one more year. You must remember; I told you all about it days ago. It's called Fairfields School. Well, Jennifer Tennison—that's Mrs. Tennison's daughter, and Mrs. Tennison calls her a little girl though she's as old as I am—well, Jennifer Tennison is at Fairfields."

"That's a coincidence," Pop agreed.

"So Mrs. Tennison thinks I ought to try to get in, too. I told her I hadn't quite made up my mind about school, and that made her laugh. She says I'm lucky if you let me make up my mind about things like that. She was that way about lots of things I said—amused and surprised, but more surprised than amused," ended Francie with mild resentment.

"Just the same, I think school's the only answer. We ought not to put it off any longer, I guess," said her father. "How about our making up our minds right now?"

"Oh gosh. All right." Francie sighed deeply.

"You've got to do something with your time, you know," continued Pop.

"I guess so, but—well, okay. I know I can't go on fooling around by myself here in London. I might get into bad habits and the wrong crowd, going to the Zoo." Francie looked slyly at her father.

"You shouldn't mind the Zoo so much. A lot of sensible people drop in there, the same way we go for a walk in the Park; it isn't strictly for kids, honey. If I only knew more young people," he said uncertainly. "It seems to me there must be some young people around, for you to meet, somewhere."

"I haven't heard Mrs. Tennison say anything about boys, all day," said Francie in glum tones. The wilting waitress had mournfully removed their plates of fish and potatoes, and brought them small single caramel eclairs. Francie eyed hers with distrust. "The food in this place is terrible, isn't it?"

"Don't be too hard on the food," Pop said. "The English probably don't like it any better than you do. But they've got the spunk to put up with it."

Hastily Francie veered away from the subject of food. "I don't think there *are* any boys in a girl's life, here in England, Pop. I don't know how the girls get around to dances or movies, but I didn't like to ask. It might look as if I wanted to know, and Mrs. Tennison might not like that."

"Probably the boys are all away at boarding school too," suggested Pop.

"It does sound awful, having to go to boarding school. Oh, Mrs. Tennison says to tell you she's asked the Fairfields people to send you a prospectus, you know, like a pamphlet, all about the school. And she says we're supposed to go to this town where it is and look at it first, and talk to the woman who runs it, before we sign up. And she says I've got to get special clothes for it; she called the outfit a uniform. I thought only orphan asylums and armies had uniforms, didn't you?" She giggled. "I hope I have to wear a lot of gold braid with it. I'll have my picture taken and send it to Ruth to show around at the Chocolate Shoppe."

"It's for less than a year, remember," said Pop. He lifted the little coffee cup the waitress had put down in front of him when she removed the eclair plate; he took a sip and made a face, in spite of his defense of the English.

"Isn't it terrible?" said Francie, who had been watching him, waiting for his reaction. "I tried it already," she added.

Pop said ruefully, "I've had it several times now, but it's always a shock."

"It's for less than a year, remember," said Francie, wagging her finger at him. She huddled her coat around her and shivered. Outside the dining-room windows, in the feeble gleam of the street light, she saw that it had begun to rain again.

One morning a few days later a letter arrived from Penelope. Francie read it aloud at the breakfast table.

" 'Dear Francie:

" 'How are you settling in? Do you absolutely hate England, or haven't you made up your mind? I've thought of you so often and wondered what's happening to you.

" 'As for me, I'm on top of the world. I needn't have been so worried. My stepfather is very nice, though quite strong-minded about things. I do believe he was more afraid of me than I was of him, and it's quite all right now. Mummy's much happier than she used to be before she met him, so even if I didn't like him I would try to, but I do, if that isn't too involved. We have spent most of our spare time getting used to each other again, Mummy and I. I'm afraid she is scandalized by my manners and ideas, but she comforts herself with the thought that school will put me straight, and transform me into a real English girl again. I may have my own ideas about this, but I'm not talking. Between you and me, I do get most awfully homesick for New Hampshire. But courage! It will be nice to see you again, and hear you talk a familiar language. By the way, Mummy's putting in a word for you at Fairfields——'

"That's two words," said Francie. "It must be awfully hard to get into the schools around here."

"I have the catalog here," said Pop.

"Not catalog, Pop, prospectus. Let's see it."

Raptly she studied the booklet, while the fried bread and tomatoes grew cold on her plate. There were handsome photographs of a large building, of tennis courts, and gardens. There were lists of subjects—she noticed that "Art" was included—and mysterious references to "Houses," and names of equally mysterious "Governors."

"A lot of teachers and not many students," she said finally. "It says here there are only fifty girls.

That will seem queer after Jefferson High; we had over two hundred there."

"You'll soon get used to it," said Mr. Nelson. "I asked Bob Tennison what we do first about this school proposition, and he says we ought to go down a time or two before you make the final move, just to talk to the headmistress and look around. That's the way they do it over here. So I'd better call these people up and see if it's all right. If it is, we might as well get you moved in right away."

As things turned out, it wasn't as simple as that. When the Nelsons went lightheartedly to inspect the school, their normal American tempo was slowed down so abruptly that they felt as if they had been brought to a complete standstill. At first sight of the school, which looked at a distance more like a gray stone farmhouse than an institute of learning, Francie felt a throb of interest. It seemed wiser, however, to conceal it; she didn't want to raise Pop's hopes too high about her future happiness.

"It's awfully different from anything I've been used to," she said, "isn't it? Prettier in a way. Jefferson High was a red brick barrack-house compared to this." She kept her tone noncommittal, but she felt excited now.

"I guess those barn-like things must be extra rooms," said Pop wisely. "Wonder how they heat the place."

"It's all terribly green outside for this time of year; maybe it's been a funny season, not cold. Are those tennis courts?"

The car they had hired at the railway station curved around the driveway and deposited them at the front door. After a long wait for the maid to answer the bell, they were ushered through a bare, high-ceilinged room with an odor familiar to Francie. "School smell," she said to herself. "The same anywhere in the world, I shouldn't wonder." A moment later they were in the imposing presence of Miss Maitland, the headmistress.

There had been nobody to warn Francie that a headmistress in England is usually an awe-inspiring person; she had come to school as unsuspectingly as a lamb to the slaughter. Now, faced with this gray-haired lady with the high coiffure, she was suddenly overwhelmed with confusion. She forgot to listen to her father. He didn't seem to be at all awed; in the midst of her unaccustomed embarrassment Francie found time to wonder at him and admire him as he chatted on and asked intelligent questions.

"Yes, of course," Pop was saying to something Miss Maitland had pronounced in her full voice about English school requirements. "Probably her Latin's way behind. But as my little girl won't attempt to pass any of your examinations. . . ."

In a normal mood, Francie would have protested being called a little girl. Even now she opened her mouth. But at the same moment she looked at Miss Maitland's face and decided to keep quiet. It was not that the headmistress looked terrifying, or even particularly severe, but she was dignified to a degree Francie had never before seen.

"I'd think twice before I sassed anybody around *her*," she told herself. "Oh dear, how can I ever live up to this place?"

At that moment Miss Maitland smiled at her with a warmth which made her seem for a moment a different person, much less forbidding. "Go and look out the windows if you'd like to, Frances, my dear," she said. "Wander about, if you're curious to see the buildings, only don't go into any room where the door is closed, because that means lessons are going on."

Gratefully Francie escaped from the drawing room, though she merely stood uncertainly in the driveway afterwards, not daring to walk about, until Pop reappeared.

"That's all right as far as I know," he said cheerfully as they drove back to the station. "A few formalities about sponsors and inquiries at the bank, and you're launched at Fairfields, chicken. How do you feel?"

"Frozen."

"It wasn't too warm indoors," he admitted, "but I liked the looks of that Miss Maitland."

"She's not bad as prison wardresses go, I suppose," said Francie in gloomy tones.

Pop came back to the hotel one evening in cheerful mood, to find his daughter waiting in his room in a state of perturbation.

"Hello," he said. "What's the matter with you? Have you been crying, or laughing too hard, or what?"

"Both. You sit down, Pop, and don't move until I come back. I've got something to show you."

"But what——"

Francie pushed him backwards, violently, to an armchair. "You just wait and be good," she said, hurrying to her own bedchamber.

When she came back, mincing like a mannequin, one hand held out with the wrist elegantly bent, he was appalled. He was really speechless for a moment.

Francie was attired in a loose gray flannel garment, bulky though sleeveless, of a pattern he had seen in charity hospitals when the patients who wore them were convalescent. Her arms were covered with blue and white striped cloth, and he realized slowly that beneath the gray flannel she was wearing an entire shirt of this material, for her neck was constricted in a collar of it, not unlike his own, held together by a blue necktie. The skirt was very short; in fact it scarcely covered her knees. She wore short socks and heavy walking shoes. On her head was a hard gray hat with a blue-striped ribbon. He could scarcely recognize his pretty daughter.

"How do I look?" she asked, pirouetting before him.

"What *is* this, anyway?" demanded Pop.

"School uniform. Fairfields uniform. We should have waited to see some of the girls before we signed up. I realize that now." Francie seemed to be in earnest, but Pop said, "I don't believe it. There must be some mistake. They'd never make you kids——"

"There's no mistake, Pop, I'm positive. I called up the store to make sure, and they told me they've provided Fairfields uniforms for years and years and years, since—oh, I don't know, since before the Battle of Hastings at least."

"Now Francie."

"Well, maybe not quite that far back, though this outfit looks like it. Honestly, Pop, isn't it terrible?"

Pop rubbed his head. "Well. . . ." He sucked at his underlip thoughtfully. "It's for less than a year," he said at last. It was a feeble remark, but the only one he could think of.

As the day approached when the gates of Fairfields would close permanently upon her, Francie found herself clinging more and more to the thought of two girls. There was Penny, of course, since she was already a friend and would be the one person in the place Francie would know. But she found herself thinking of Jennifer Tennison as well, wondering about her, hoping that she would be a friend too, even feeling that, in a way, she knew Jennifer, having heard so much about her from her mother. True, Mrs. Tennison had referred to her daughter sickeningly as "my little girl," but, even allowing for a doting mother's prejudice, Jennifer sounded rather a good sort. Besides, Pop had been feeding her Jennifer at every other breath for days now. He was always quoting Bob Tennison on the subject of his daughter and predicting that Francie and Jennifer would be buddies of the heart-to-heart sort.

At any other time Francie might have resisted such heavy-handed enthusiasm. But now she was lonely for the company of those her own age, and she began to build up Jennifer in her imagination as another Penelope, but even more so. Francie, who was used to more friends than she knew how to count, was ready to reach in the dark for almost anyone who was young and lively and interested in something besides ancient tombs and modern zoos.

Thus she was fully prepared to like Jennifer when she met her. She was anything but ready for the way Jennifer was so well prepared *not* to like her.

Their first encounter came in the dormitory on Francie's first night at Fairfields. Pop had brought her out in the evening after dinner, so that she could settle in for the night with the other girls and be ready to step right into school routine in the morning.

FRANCIE

Miss Maitland had assigned Penelope the task of helping Francie get settled and Penny had been wonderful. She'd made everything seem quite simple and pleasant, what with introducing her around, showing her her bed in the dormitory, helping her unpack. Apparently Penny herself had fitted in as comfortably as though she'd never left England. Already, Francie noted, some of her Americanisms were being replaced by English terms, and the other girls had accepted her readily enough. But they were holding back a bit, as far as Francie was concerned, stiffly polite, not quite ready to make the American girl one of themselves.

Their attitude surprised Francie. There'd been an English exchange student at Jefferson once and every girl in school had fallen over herself trying to extend the well-known "hand across the sea." That these English girls should not welcome her as quickly puzzled Francie and made her a little self-conscious.

That was probably why she made the remark she did about her bed. The Sixth Form girls didn't all sleep in one room, exactly; each girl had a little cubicle marked off from the others by an arrangement of curtains. Francie had just been introduced to her special cell, and to show her good will had bounced cheerfully on the bed. To her surprise, there was no responding give of good old American innersprings; just a resisting plop that jarred her to the teeth.

"My gosh!" cried Francie. "Do you actually sleep on these prison pallets?"

A hush fell upon the dormitory and Francie, quickly sensitive, knew that it was the hostile silence of those offended. It was then she noticed a girl who had just come into the dormitory and was standing in the aisle a short distance away. She was a stocky, youngish-looking girl with pale blue eyes and sandy hair. But the surprising thing was the scornful way in which she was staring directly at Francie.

"I'd always heard how soft you Yanks are," the girl said.

Francie, not believing her ears, stared back. "Yanks? *Who's* a Yank?"

The other girl tossed her limp hair free of one shoulder. "I shouldn't wonder if you are, Nelson."

"Oh hush, Jennifer!" said Penelope crossly. "Francie's not a Yankee—she's from the Middle West. And these beds *are* hard."

Jennifer, Francie thought unhappily. This unappealing-looking girl with the sharp tongue and the resentment against Americans was the "buddy" she was to have taken to her heart. Instead of being wildly angry as she would have been at home, Francie experienced only a weary, letdown feeling. So this was the English reserve she had heard so much about—this frozen silence all around her. Well, let them be that way! She could be reserved too.

FRANCIE

Without glancing in Jennifer's direction again, even ignoring Penny, who was trying her best to ease the awkwardness, Francie got ready for bed. Not till "lights out" did she relax her stony, vigilant guard. Then she lay stiffly on the hard, unfamiliar bed, hating England and Fairfields and especially Jennifer, aching with longing for home and her own kind.

Back home in Jefferson a letter had arrived from Francie Nelson, and Ruth could hardly wait to get on the telephone.

"Gretta?" she cried excitedly into the receiver. "I've just got a letter from Francie and it's going to kill you. The poor thing."

"I suppose she's coming back soon," said Gretta gloomily, "before Prom."

"Oh no, not at all. No such luck for Francie; on the contrary she's all set at school over there. It's a boarding school at that."

"Boarding school?" Gretta sounded more cheerful now. "Read it to me, why don't you, if it's not too long."

"Well, I won't go through all the guff on the first two pages because it's sort of hysterical. It's about her uniform."

"Uniform?"

"It's what they've got to wear at these schools, evidently," explained Ruth. "She says she tried to get by without wearing one of these terrible outfits, pleading that textile shortage they're always talking about in the English papers. But Miss Maitland, who's the headmistress—that's a sort of principal—said she thought it advisable to look like the others, which means she thought it necessary, so poor Francie's running around looking like a female convict, and playing hockey."

"Well, go on," Gretta said. "What else?"

"Here's what she writes," Ruth said. " 'This Miss Maitland is what I might call a sourpuss, but we haven't got a lot to do with her, luckily, as she scares me to death. She takes some of the girls for Latin, but I'm so far behind in Latin they've given me up in despair. I'm not trying for any of their University examinations so they don't really care. People don't graduate here. There's something about certificates instead, and because everybody knows I'm only here for a while they don't worry. But they're way ahead of me in most things; I was surprised to find out how far I've had to go back to the younger girls' forms—that means classes—for maths and French and goodness knows what, and if I can catch up, entrance exams into State won't bother me a bit. In the meantime, though, it makes me awfully ashamed to seem so dumb.

" 'As for social life outside the school, there isn't any. They think men are but poison, when they admit their existence at all. Even when I write to Glenn—' " Ruth paused until Gretta's exaggerated groans had died out on the telephone, and continued without comment— " 'when I write to Glenn

I feel terribly guilty and hide the address. I don't think they'd go so far as to censor our letters but I don't trust Miss Maitland. Sometimes I figure I might as well be in a nunnery. The funny thing is, I'm getting used to it.' "

Ruth paused again as a sound of disbelief came over the phone from Gretta.

"I don't think she'll last the time out," said Gretta, plunged in stubborn gloom. "I'm sure I couldn't. I'm not sure I'd wish this fate even on Francie Nelson. What else does she say?"

"Not very much more, except that the way she's feeling right now, the fur coat her father promised her when she gets back has got to be something really snazzy. No mouton or rabbit. Oh yes, and that this girl she met on the boat—Penny her name is—is a great comfort, being half human because she was over here so long. But there's another girl——"

A decidedly angry voice broke in. It belonged to Ruth's mother on the telephone extension. "Now girls, you'll simply have to hang up. I've waited as long as I'm going to; I've got to get through to the grocery store."

"Call you later, Gretta," said Ruth resignedly. There were times, she knew, when even a mother must be allowed to assert herself.

It was the third week of term, and the Fairfields girls were taking their morning run, scattering out on the driveway as they emerged from the school door. It was not yet eight o'clock, and still dark. Under the clouded sky the trees of Fairfields' famous oak park very slowly took on shape and solidity. The air was cold but not crisp; there was a hint of rain in it.

Francie lowered her head and ran glumly, sniffling as she went. She wore no makeup and her hair was arranged for simplicity, not chic. She looked several years younger and several degrees less contented. She seemed always to have a cold these days; not a very bad one but nothing very comfortable either. The sniffle waxed and waned and never quite went away. Nobody paid any attention to colds at Fairfields unless a girl ran a temperature and complained of sore throat. Just now, for example, everybody in Francie's House had a cold, severe or mild. Even Penelope had one, though she was usually adaptable to climates.

"Hi there." It was Penny herself trotting along next to Francie. She ran lightly, without noticeable puffing. "How you doing?" she continued, and Francie noted that she was already losing her American accent in spite of an occasional noble effort to keep it.

"I'm doing all right. At least," said Francie, "these days I don't want to die before we get back to the Hall, as I did at first. I'm beginning to think I'll live through the whole experience."

"That's the spirit. Chin up."

The games mistress, who was leading the herd,

now blew her whistle, which was a signal for the girls to wheel about and start back toward the school. Daylight was growing stronger now; the slanting lines of mist thinned out. It was a maddening mist which Francie could never get used to; looked at from indoors it was exactly like a fine rain, yet out of doors one couldn't feel separate drops of water. There was just a general clamminess everywhere, all the time. Still, she reflected, one shouldn't complain about England's climate. What was the use? There it was, and in a way it was a good climate; nowhere else had she seen such rich green grass and beautiful trees. That was the rain's doing. Jefferson's countryside seemed parched and brown when she thought of it.

"Going to be—a good—day," said Penny, panting now as she jogged along, for the girls' pace had been quickened by the games mistress who led them, as they approached the big front door.

"That won't do me much good. I'm still way behind in maths and today I've got to swot."

"Pity," said Penny, who was quick at mathematics. "I do wish I could give you a hand. Still, you have it easy in your turn when it comes to history, and I'm no good at that. . . . Home at last." She puffed out her cheeks. "Just in time, too; I'm dying for brekker."

The girls filed into the refectory in a general symphony of sniffling, nose-blowing and throat-clearing. Surveying her companions Francie was struck, as usual, by their luxuriant tresses worn in many stages of disarray. There wasn't what she considered a well-groomed head in the room. Hair at school wasn't an adornment at all, but a nuisance.

Francie, looking around her at the table, suddenly realized that she was beginning to feel a part of the group that filled the dining hall. They looked a nice crowd of girls. They weren't unglamorous strangers as they had seemed at first, but pleasant enough creatures. She felt a surge of affection for them, though no doubt that was due in part to relief at being back in the building, sitting down at table, instead of still trotting about in the slanting lines of dank mist. Everyone looked nice this morning, even Miss Turner. This week she was at Miss Turner's table; there was a mistress presiding at each, and the girls moved around from one table to the next, every week. Miss Turner had been their chaperone in the train at the beginning of term—what the girls called a "traveling aunt." She was stiff and humorless and usually difficult. This morning, however, for the first time, Francie did not hate her.

Nevertheless a familiar thought assailed her. "What am I doing here?" she asked herself. How strange were the ways of Fate! She thought of morning coffee in Aunt Norah's breakfast nook, with Ruth dropping in early to pick her up for school, drinking a glass of orange juice with her at the little red-lacquered table between the benches.

FRANCIE

The sun was coming in through the red-checked curtains at the kitchen window. The Frigidaire sang its happy little song, that humming buzz of America that has taken the place of the outdated teakettle singing away on the hob. It was hot, but not as hot as it would be by nine o'clock when it was time to go to school. Ruth and she were giggling about something they had seen at the movies the night before. Francie was wearing black shoes like ballet slippers and—let's see, what would she be wearing? Her plaid skirt and white blouse, perhaps. . . . She was just reaching for that American glass of orange juice when she recovered herself with a slight start.

The Jefferson breakfast nook was far away. She was sitting at a refectory table in damp, dark, dank England, spooning up the last of her porridge, which was eaten without milk. She was dressed like all the other girls there, but there was nothing soldier-like or smart in these depressing gray costumes. If the idea was to make them all look alike, she reflected, it was a theory that failed in practice; the more they stuck to the pattern the more the individual stood out as unusually leggy, or dumpy, or curly-haired, or gray-eyed. Some of the girls wore mousy brown braids and some had bushy manes of reddish gold.

Perhaps the thing hardest to get used to, she reflected as she had done many times before, was the youth of these girls. It was shocking to Francie that they should be such *babies*. Not in years: most of the girls in her own form were more or less of an age with her. It was their attitude toward life. The whole thing was so completely different from anything she had known that her pen failed her when she tried to tell Ruth or Glenn about it in a letter.

"Maybe it's partly that we oldest ones are only a handful compared to the rest of the school," she had written to Glenn, "and that the little kids are only twelve. It's been a long time since I spent much time in a crowd with a lot of twelve-year-olds and so forth. But they know their place; the ages don't exactly mingle except when we play some of the games. Only I give you my word, I wouldn't know how old some of these girls in my dorm are if I had to guess. They're as old as I am, but they prattle like nursery-school inmates. I feel like a nurse sometimes. You ought to hear them in the dorm."

She chuckled to herself now as she thought of some of the bedtime conversations they had. The girls chatted freely through the flimsy walls of their cubicle curtains and often the evening air rang with eager discussions of games, history lessons, and rudimentary religious topics. There was never a word of parties or boys or dresses, or any of the topics Francie's Jefferson crowd would have chosen.

"They're subnormal," said Francie to herself. "I'm spending what should be my formative years with a lot of subnormal kids."

Then because she didn't want to be always whining, even to herself, she pulled up. They were nice girls—healthy, tomboy, nice girls. It was not their fault that they should remind Francie so fatally of her playmates at the summer camp she had attended when she was twelve. If the truth were known, she didn't really mind feeling superior; she admitted that to herself wryly. "I may be compensating for the people who snub me," she thought. "Anyway in their fashion some of them are clever. Gwen's good at music. Heaps of them are better than I'll ever be at tennis."

But it was Penelope, of course, who got on best with the American—Penelope, whose blue eyes were reflective and kind, and who was able to skip with enviable nimbleness from American to British mentality, and back again. The worst girl in the place, the only real trial, thought Francie, as she drained her mug of sweetened tea, was Jennifer Tennison. But prayers were beginning, and she must stand with the others behind her chair, with hanging head. The glow of their morning exercise was fading; she shivered. Somebody near her sniffled. Someone across the room coughed.

Prayers finished, Miss Maitland up at the head table began to read the day's notices. Francie's feet were numb. Her spirits took a dive downward as her body grew colder; she forgot the girls and the new, if fleeting, feeling of comradeship. She felt too low to think about Ruth or Glenn or the hot morning sun of Jefferson. She didn't listen to Miss Maitland's voice, except to wait for the word of dismissal.

She kept saying to herself, "I'm in prison. It's no use trying to cheer up; this is exactly like a prison. Pop couldn't have known it would be as bad as this."

CHAPTER 5

THE GIRLS came out the way the animals went into the Ark, two by two. In the corridor they broke ranks to disperse at a run for class. It was in the corridor that Francie, still in a mood, encountered the person she most disliked in the whole school, the person who, presumably and logically, should have been her best friend—Jennifer Tennison. She caught her breath in annoyance and apprehension. She saw Jennifer repeatedly, every day, all day, first thing in the morning and last thing at night, but she never learned to relax about it.

Sometimes Penny tried to reason with Francie about this difficulty in her new life. "Why let her get you down?" Penny would say. "It's only what she's trying to do, and the more you allow it the worse she'll get, the little drip."

"I'm not used to it, that's all. Nobody's ever been so mean to me before—anyway not unless I gave them some cause," added Francie with a sudden memory of Gretta and a few others. "But Jennifer started it and she's been at it ever since the first night here. Why, do you suppose?" She stared with honest pained bewilderment at her friend.

"Suppose we try to figure out why," said Penelope. "There's a reason for everything . . . What makes one girl mean to another, usually?"

"Well, usually," said Francie in thoughtful tones, "it's jealousy. At least, it was always jealousy as far as I was concerned . . . and I'm not bragging." She broke off and looked carefully over her shoulder. "You know that, don't you, Penny? It might sound like boasting, but *you* know what I mean. I told you about all that—Jefferson and the parties and being popular. You're the only one in the whole school who would understand."

She sounded plaintive, but Penny did indeed understand, and said so. "However, that theory doesn't get us anywhere in this case," continued the English girl, with the reflective air Francie so much liked and admired. "You haven't grabbed any of Jennifer's boy friends—if they exist, which is doubtful—and even if your clothes are nicer than hers she can't possibly resent it as we only wear uniforms here. What do *you* think, yourself? Is there anything you may have said, or done, without thinking?"

"N-no, not that I know of. But I'll tell you what," Francie lowered her voice and peered through the curtains of her cubicle to make sure they were not overheard. As Jennifer lived in the same dormitory, they got little chance of talking out of her hearing; they got little privacy altogether, and the two newcomers agreed that was one of the aspects of school life that they found most trying. "I'll tell you what," continued Francie. "Maybe her people did just what Pop did to me, and insisted too much on what friends we were bound to be. Pop gave me Jennifer Tennison for breakfast, lunch and dinner every day for weeks before I met her. Of course, not having friends here, it worked all right with me and in the beginning I was ready to like her. But it might have had just the opposite effect with her if the Tennisons did the same thing."

"That could be how it started," said Penelope. "As for the rest—oh well, they say there's a bully in every school, and though Jennifer can't very well twist your arm, there are other ways."

"You're telling me!" said Francie.

Now, in the corridor, she bristled instinctively at the sight of Jennifer. Yet Jennifer's first words were friendly enough. "Hullo, Francie," she said, pausing.

"Hullo, Jennifer."

They stood there regarding each other, two girls in gray flannel uniforms, much of an age. It might have surprised a casual onlooker to know that one saw the other as a snake coiling for the strike.

"Finding your maths any easier going?" asked Jennifer. Like Penelope, she was very good at mathematics. Unlike Penelope she was always reminding other people of it.

"I try, but it's awfully hard," said the incautious Francie.

Jennifer fell back a pace, registering extreme astonishment. "Oh, never. Surely not! Yanks are always frightfully good at sums. They're wonderful at adding up dollars and all that sort of thing, aren't they, Hardcastle?"

Wendy Hardcastle, appealed to in full flight as she swept through the hall, paused a second. She smiled vaguely. "Do stop pulling her leg," she implored in high sweet tones, and hurried on.

"You Yanks——" continued Jennifer.

"I'm not a Yankee, Jennifer, I've told you so a dozen times! Yankees come from New England. I'm from the Middle West." Francie was going through the familiar struggle of trying to keep her temper. She always tried, and usually failed.

Jennifer hesitated, searching her mind for some other remark that would be offensive but not crude. But her spite was not alert enough; time was pressing and girls were hurrying past them, reminding them of work. Francie escaped, therefore, without more insults being shot at her for the moment. She made her way to the history class with her nose in the air and her cheeks burning. *Why* should that girl be so nasty? It made everything in this horrid school seem much horrider. There wasn't any sense to it.

"Oh, if I could only take a recording of that female, and play it for Pop!" she thought. "If he only knew half the things she says, he'd probably break off business relations with her father." She might, of course, write a letter to Pop and tell him about it, but she couldn't consider that. It was the sort of thing one didn't do. Back in America the girls and boys talked about their differences when they came home in the evening; it had seemed natural somehow. But boarding school was different, Francie realized. Here, she was very much a member of her own group, in her own world. It wasn't the world of parents; all that was completely foreign to Fairfields. One was polite to adults or to children, but they belonged to different castes and were kept in their places. One didn't confide in people "outside."

"These kids are a tight, exclusive little band," Francie thought ruefully, "just the kind of exclusiveness I don't like, and yet here I am, one of them!"

However, whether she liked it or not she had to obey the moral code, and this was impossible to explain, even to herself. She only knew that she mustn't tell. Neither Pop nor Mr. Tennison must be told that Jennifer was such a thorn in her side. Partly, of course, the reason for her silence was that she didn't want to be laughed at. No parent would be able to see how annoying these pinpricks could be. After all, whatever Jennifer did never sounded as bad as it was. How could one explain the unrelenting persecution of it? Taking each one separately the spiteful remarks were trivial.

The very first morning, for instance, when Francie had innocently said, "I won't wash yet; I'll wait until the water gets warm," Jennifer had pounced on her words, hooted with scornful mirth, and made the whole dormitory laugh at the American for a luxurious fool who expected warm water. At odd moments Jennifer, for want of other material for annoyance, could always crack down on her for saying "ca-an't" instead of "cahn't," or put on a high nasal whine as if in imitation of an American accent. She also seemed to hold Francie personally responsible for the history and foreign policy of the United States.

"During the war——" Francie might begin in all innocence, and Jennifer was on her in a moment.

"The war, did you say? Oh, do tell us about it, Francie. We don't know anything about it over here in England, of course. We'd like to hear all about your experiences in Chicago. It must have been absolutely *frightful*. You were killed by a bomb, no doubt. Go on, Francie, you needn't be shy."

All Francie could retort to an attack like that was a feeble, "I don't live in Chicago." Afterwards, of course, she had the most violent fits of rage, when Jennifer was gone beyond the range of influence. She could think of good cutting remarks when it was too late. But in Jennifer's presence she couldn't do anything.

"Why don't you stand up to her?" urged Penelope.

"I don't know how to," said Francie miserably. "I don't see why she *should* be so anti-American. I get so puzzled I can't talk. Doesn't she know her father works with mine in London? Mr. Tennison has an interest in Pop's company; the Americans and the British work their oil wells together in that firm."

Penny said, "That wouldn't make any difference to Jennifer; she probably thinks her father rather low, you see, because he's in trade."

Francie blinked. "I don't get it."

"It's just a silly English idea," said Penny, "though it's sort of dying out nowadays; after all, anybody who can make a go of trade today is jolly lucky as well as clever. But Tennison's a silly ass; she's taken that attitude and she holds by it. At least that's what I'm beginning to think."

"Trade," said Francie thoughtfully. "I thought that meant selling things for other things—swapping, you know."

"So it does, but the way they use the word here in England, it means shops. Selling groceries or motorcars, or, I suppose, oil, the way your father and Tennison's do."

"Then *everybody's* in trade, as well as our fathers," said Francie. "I still don't catch."

"Everybody is, in America, if you don't count teachers or football players or actors or interior decorators," said Penny, laughing. "And it's the same here except that rather a lot of men are in the Army or Navy."

"So are they in the States, but they don't boast about it especially."

"Well, they're rather proud of it here," said Penny, jumping to her feet as the class bell rang, "so I suppose that proves you're more modest in America, with better manners. Anyway, don't take Tennison too seriously. She'll get her neck rung one of these days if she doesn't grow less poisonous."

Books under their arms, they hurried down the hall. "I'll try not to let her get me down," Francie said. "I haven't any time to worry about her; I'm too busy hating the rest of the setup to concentrate so much on Jennifer."

Penny glanced at her with concern. "Is it really so bad as all that?"

"It's not so good," Francie admitted. "I don't tell anybody but you of course, but I'm *cold*. I'm *never* warm or cozy. And everything's so awfully different. . . . Well, I'll be seeing you."

Penny must have given the matter serious thought; she sought out Francie later when the lessons for the day were done and the girls were taking their "P.T.," as they called physical training.

"I say, Nelson, I feel responsible for your misery. I am sorry. After all, if it hadn't been for me you might never have come to Fairfields."

"Oh no, Penny, Pop had made up his mind I'd have to go to school before we ever talked to you, so you can stop worrying. I guess any English school would offer problems of some sort—to me, anyway. I didn't mean to complain."

"But Francie, don't you like anything at all about England? Don't you care for the countryside, for out-of-doors?" asked Penelope wistfully. "I'd hate to think you were hating us. I did have such a wizard time in the States."

"Oh, of course there's a whole lot of England I like. I love the riding more than anything. I exaggerated; I'm just homesick, I guess." Francie sighed. "To be absolutely frank with you, Penelope, I miss all the boys, that's what's worrying me most. Don't you ever want a date? Why are all these girls so, well, indifferent to dates and men and all that? Why, you know perfectly well that any female back home who didn't have her Saturday night date just wouldn't rate at all."

Penelope's face took on the uneasy expression that Francie had learned to associate at Fairfields with any mention of dating.

"Yes, I know. But they don't go in for all that until later on, in England," she said. "Not until school's over, or anyway only during hols. Thinking very much about boys is soppy. That's how the English look at it."

Francie said in amazement, "But that's absolutely mad! What's wrong with boys? Why, half the world is boys!"

"*I* know," said Penny, "but they don't think of that. It—it's just considered soppy."

"What's soppy? What's wrong with dates? In Jefferson——"

"It's different here, Francie. It's no use arguing with *me* about it; I didn't make the rules. I'm only trying to explain the difference," said Penelope reasonably. "I don't mean girls here live in a nunnery, necessarily. We go to parties sometimes; we dance with men. Only, as long as we're at school we're supposed to keep our minds on—shhhh." The games mistress had blown her whistle shrilly, demanding silence. The girls all stood at attention.

Suddenly there came a break in the austere routine. As a special treat for having got the highest scholastic average, Francie's form was allowed to go up to town, to attend a production of *Richard the Third*. Her classmates were wildly excited at the prospect, and Francie herself was interested, though she would have liked to be blasé. "After all it is something to see a first-class English Shakespeare production," she admitted to herself.

To her shocked chagrin, she found that the girls were expected to wear their uniforms for the expedition; it nearly spoiled the entire idea for fastidious Miss Nelson. But since none of the others seemed to dread appearing like that in the great metropolis, Francie allowed herself to be comforted. It wasn't as if Glenn or any of the other men in her life would be there to see her, anyway. (She giggled as she thought of their faces if they could witness one of the school outings.) Their traveling aunt for the day was to be Miss West, a rather prim member of the staff. Francie learned the other details from the girls' excited talk. They would catch the ten o'clock train for London, and that meant changing trains once on the way. They would arrive just in time for luncheon before the matinée, and it would be a scramble then to catch the five-forty-five train down to the country and school again.

"Lunch in a restaurant will be great fun," said Wendy Hardcastle, her face shining with naïve hope. "I hope it'll be a decent one; I do get fed up with this eternal Thames mud and worms we get."

Francie, having long since learned that these words referred to chocolate custard and spaghetti, merely said gloomily, "It'll be awful wherever we go. I was hungry all the time when we were staying in London at the hotel."

"Oh yes, isn't the food *frightful* in those places?" said Wendy agreeably. "Mummy says she simply hates staying in town."

"The chief snag is, there's nothing to do about it," said another girl. "One place is as bad as another, even the posh hotels."

"That's exactly it." Francie spoke eagerly. "At home in Jefferson, we can always fill up somehow, at the corner drugstore or somewhere. We can go in anywhere and order a double malted, practically any time of the day. Here, if you asked for a double malted nobody would know what you meant. Even if you ask for a glass of plain milk——"

"There was a war, Yank," said Jennifer. "We didn't have the time America had to stock up on food; we were busy defending you people."

At that moment something happened to Francie. She felt as if all the warm blood in her body had rushed to her head; she heard herself saying in a tired voice, which managed to be very rude though it was quiet, "Oh, do shut up, Jennifer. Nobody was defending anything but himself and his own rights in the war, so do shut up, will you? I'm *so* fed up with all that gup you give out with all the time."

Certainly it was strange, and a stranger thing happened then: Jennifer actually did shut up. The other girls looked at each other in amusement.

"That's the stuff to give the troops, Francie," said Wendy approvingly. "It doesn't do any harm to show your teeth once in a while."

Francie flushed with surprise and pleasure.

Westers, as the girls disrespectfully called their traveling aunt behind her back, decreed when they set forth for their treat that there was to be no special visiting of relatives in London on anyone's part, since there was no time for it. Aunts, cousins, even fathers living in the city would only interfere with the program, and must be ignored.

"After all, you saw your people, most of you, at half-term," she said. "Frances' father has very kindly written to ask if he can't give us all lunch"—the girls cheered shrilly—"but I'm sure he wouldn't enjoy it," she went on firmly, "in the time available, so we have thanked him and refused. Some other time when we're not so rushed, Frances, I'm sure we would love it, and it's *most* kind and noble of him to have suggested it. Most men would be terrified."

"That's quite all right, Miss West," Francie replied. "It's not important."

Nor was it, for distances in England seemed very small to her. A trip of sixty miles or so to London was, after all, nothing to an American girl.

"He'll probably invite us again some other time," she added.

"I do hope so," said Miss West. "We're so fond of your father, and it was thoughtful of him to arrange that that ham be sent. All the way from his office in New York, think of it! We are lucky; I don't suppose there's another school where they've had their fill of ham, for ages."

"I'm not so frightfully keen on ham," murmured Jennifer.

"No? Then why did you gobble yours the day we had it, and ask for more?" asked Penny, pouncing.

"Now, girls."

They rode in to catch the train in the school station wagon, which Francie had learned to call a "utility brake," though she couldn't get used to the words. There were eight of them, nine if you counted Miss West, and when the train steamed in to the platform and they climbed aboard, it was discovered that there were no completely empty carriages. Therefore the girls had to distribute themselves throughout the coach. They giggled and whispered in the process as if, thought Francie a bit sourly, they were straight out of kindergarten. She felt agonizingly conspicuous. She had no doubt that everyone on the train was looking at her, thinking she had no more sense than these other badly-dressed chits. With cold deliberation she hung on to Penny's arm; Penny was all right; she could be trusted to act like a lady instead of snickering and bouncing about in a childish manner. If observers *should* happen to look again at those two, after their first disgusted glance at the whole party, they might realize that here at least were two young women who knew how to behave in public. Haughtily Francie sat down in the carriage Penny found, and tried to pull her skimpy skirt further over her knees.

The train gathered speed. In another compartment, she knew, Westers was sitting with two of the other girls, reading *The Spectator*. She had seen them settled in before finding her own seat. Penny and Francie were sharing their carriage with a man in naval uniform and a middle-aged woman with a kerchief on her head. For all her good intentions to retain an adult dignity, Francie's high spirits began to get the better of her; it was exciting, after all these weeks, to be on her way somewhere, and outside the train windows the sun, for a wonder, was actually shining down on the green fields. The girls began to whisper and laugh; and the kerchiefed woman smiled in sympathy. Out of the corner of her eyes Francie saw the naval officer smile. It wasn't a broad grin, but it was definitely a smile.

The train stopped at the next station and the woman got out. As they started up again, the man leaned forward. "Off to London for a spree?" he asked.

"Yes," said Francie readily, glad to be asked, "we're going to see *Richard the Third*."

"It's *most* exciting," added Penelope, who loved the theater with passion. "I can hardly wait."

"It's very well done," said the naval officer. "I saw it last week."

"We were lucky to get tickets," said Francie, "it's such a hit."

"You're Yanks, aren't you?"

"Not her," said Francie, indicating Penny. "Only me."

"I'd have said you both were. I know the States very well," said the man.

Eagerly Francie explained about Penny and her ghost of an American accent. She had to do all the talking, for Penny had suddenly become quiet and ceased to speak for herself. This would have struck

Francie as odd if she had noticed, but her attention was taken up with this man who knew her country.

"Quite adventurous," he said when she told him about her visit in England. "You don't find it all easy going, do you?"

"Well——" It was on the tip of her tongue to pour out all her troubles, but just before she spoke Francie happened to glance at Penelope. Penelope was looking stiff, practically frozen. Whatever ailed her, Francie wondered; was there something about this man she herself hadn't noticed? "It's not so bad," said Francie vaguely. "What do you say, Penny?"

"Oh, not bad. Not bad at all," said Penny. She seemed to thaw just a little. "I was afraid to come back at first," she admitted. "I remembered things that would take a lot of getting used to all over again, especially the winter—windows never fitting and all that."

"Ah yes," said the naval officer, laughing. "That central heating you have over in the States; it's a shocking thing the way it undermines one's morale."

"But after the first few days," continued Penny, "I didn't notice discomforts any more. All my earlier experience came to the rescue, I suppose."

The officer told them something of his own experiences in Boston and New York. They were in the middle of an animated conversation about some of their favorite movie stars when suddenly there came a peremptory knock on the glass of the corridor door.

"Francie! Girls!"

Apparently paralyzed by horror Miss West was unable to slide back the door for herself. She could only call through the glass. It was the sober-faced Penny who got there first and opened it, though the man was close behind her to help. Whatever ailed Miss West, however, the traveling aunt was determined to control herself. She said in chilly-sweet tones, "You may join us in our carriage now, girls; there is plenty of room."

"Oh, is there? Good." Francie jumped up. "Well, it's certainly been swell meeting you," she said to the navy man over her shoulder. To her surprise, he looked amused and winked at her in conspiratorial fashion. For the first time, Francie realized all might not be well for herself.

Miss West led them back to her carriage, her face grim.

"Whatever's the matter with old sourpuss?" whispered Francie to Penelope behind her.

"We were talking to a strange man," Penny said. "I knew we shouldn't have, but I got so interested. It's not allowed, you know."

"But what possible harm——" Francie began, only to have her friend shush her as they reached their seats opposite Miss West. The other girls were silent. Miss West was silent. Perforce, Francie and

Penelope were silent, and that uneasy silence remained until the train pulled into London and Miss West had to scurry about to round up her flock. Once only during the ride had Francie caught the eye of Wendy Hardcastle; Wendy rolled her eyes to heaven and grimaced.

Off the train and hurrying toward the barrier where the tickets were collected, Francie hung back in order to apologize for the crime she had evidently committed. She was really innocent, not knowing she had done anything wrong. It wasn't, Francie fumed, as if the naval officer had been cheeky or anything; he hadn't tried to pick her up; he'd behaved like an uncle. And even if he *had* tried to pick her up, reflected Francie, she was old enough to take care of herself. Nevertheless something was obviously very much the matter with old Westers. . . .

"I'm awfully sorry, Miss West," she began, "but I didn't mean to do anything wrong. Why, at home in Jefferson——"

"That will do, Frances; this is neither the time nor the place for a talk. We'll discuss your extraordinary behavior later, if you don't mind."

Francie gasped. Never in her life had she been so snubbed; it was like falling into icy water. Her face burned and she had to swallow vigorously; from sheer shock she was about to burst into tears right there in the station, in front of all the other girls. She battled fiercely to avoid this last humiliation. By the time she had caught up with the group she had won the battle; her tears were blinked back.

All chattering and laughing except Francie, they made their way to the restaurant Miss West had chosen, and started on their lunch. Francie tried to eat. She stared at her plate in dumb agony, her mind far away. Once she glanced up and caught Penelope's gaze from the other end of the table; Penny looked as chastened as though she and Francie had really done something wrong. And after that Francie felt even worse.

Oh dear, why had she ever come to England? How could she bear to remain, after this? Her companions were such fatuous little idiots, too—their chattering, high voices rang in her ears as they spoke in their jargon that had only recently become comprehensible to her.

"Anyone want some booze?"

"Bags I. With you with that squash!"

"Buzz the bread along, will you, Wendy?"

"Thanks a ton. I say, what super chicken!"

In the middle of the last course—watery ice cream—something seemed to hit the American like a sledge hammer. She wasn't Francie any more; she was just a burning impulse to get away from Miss West and the girls. Hardly realizing what she did, she bolted from the table and out toward the entrance. Taken by surprise, Miss West could only watch her flight. No doubt she thought Francie had gone to the lavatory to have a good cry; at any rate she turned back to her flock without trying to pursue the one erring lamb.

Francie ran down the Strand, past the jumbled shop windows, making detours around people who were in less of a hurry than she was—girls in tweed coats, men carrying attaché cases, families with children; they glanced wonderingly at the girl running along the city street as if her life depended on haste.

Fortunately she could remember her father's office address. When an empty taxi nearly ran over her she hailed it and fell into its shabby leather seat. She paid the fare from her pocket money, which, as were the other girls, she was carrying tied in her handkerchief, and then she ran into the office, right past the reception clerk. If Pop wasn't there, she resolved, she would sit down and wait, even if it took hours for him to come back.

Pop was there, just about to go out to a late lunch. His mind was on oil and its international distribution. He blinked in surprise to see his daughter walk quickly through the door, her school hat pushed back on her head and her eyes red with tears.

"Why, hello, honey. I thought you weren't going to——"

She blurted out, "Pop, listen, I can't bear it any more, I can't, honestly! Let me go back home." She sat down in the nearest chair and cried openly. Her father began to speak, changed his mind, and lit a cigar instead, keeping his eyes turned away from Francie until she had stopped sobbing.

"Now then," he said, "let's have it. What's happened?"

"We came up to London for that treat, you know, *Richard the Third*."

"Yes," said Pop. "I remember. Why aren't you there with the others?"

"Well, on the train——" She told him the whole story of her gay but innocent conversation with the naval officer, trying to describe fully the unreasonable attitude of Miss West. But her words seemed inadequate; she couldn't express the true humiliation of that scene on the station platform. Her voice died out plaintively.

"Well now," said Francie's father after a pause, tipping off his cigar ash. "It seems to me you've been a little hasty, Francie. That teacher didn't understand the way you look at things, that's so, but you didn't give her much of a chance. After all, she was doing her job, and she does have to stick by the rules. Now why don't you go back and have a good long——"

"It isn't only old West," she cried impulsively. "It's everything. I hate it all, I really do, Pop. Why can't I go home? I know Aunt Norah isn't there but I could stay with Ruth till she got back. Please let me, Pop, *please*."

"I knew you were a little bit spoiled," said Pop slowly, "but I never knew you were a quitter."

"I'm not!" cried Francie in loud tones. "You

don't dare call me a quitter!" The last vestige of tears was gone from her eyes; she was furious. But Pop was angry too, in a cold way. She had never seen him so angry before.

"I don't know what else you'd call it," he said. "The very first time you run into a little disagreeableness, you turn around and beat it. What is that if it isn't quitting?"

"It's the *system*," protested Francie, twisting her hands together. "It's all so new. And they never give in one inch. They're always so sure they're right. They——"

"All right, all right, so they think they know it all. What of it? Can't you understand that attitude? Don't you ever stop to think *you* might be wrong, sometimes? Now listen, Francie." He put down his cigar and leaned over the desk, talking earnestly. In spite of her troubles, Francie was impressed.

"An American ought to know his way around everywhere," said Pop. "We've got people from all over, in our country. They make up our towns and our schools and our churches and everything else. So we ought to be really understanding of the other fellow."

"But——"

Pop swept on. "Now here you are, an American girl, who's had all the advantages and opportunities possible. You've grown up in a nation that owes a great deal to other countries. And yet the first time you come bang up against one of these other countries you get surprised and hurt. Why? What did you expect? A whole world full of Americans? Americans still have many things to learn. Remember that. You can learn some of those things here—there couldn't be a better teacher than England."

He paused and Francie hung her head, thinking it over.

"Not just tolerance of other people, honey—understanding. Don't forget, a lot of them are trying to understand us, too. Sometimes, I suspect, that makes hard going. There's another thing. After you understand people, it isn't long before you respect them, too. Try it on the English, Francie."

In the silence, Pop's desk clock ticked loudly.

"Getting along with the other fellow on his grounds—that's good manners, Francie," Pop said. "That's the best kind of manners you can have. I suspect it's something you need to learn—badly."

Francie blew her nose again, without comment.

"Now the next question is how to get you back to your party," said Pop briskly. "What time does this show of yours start? Two-thirty?"

Francie nodded.

"We'd better get over to that theater right now," Pop said, pushing back his chair and standing up. "Come on. Your Miss West must be pretty worried about you. I expect she'll be phoning here as soon as she gets the girls settled in. We'll try to beat her to it. If you look at it from her point of view, she's had a hard day herself."

"If you want to look at it from her point of view," admitted Francie. "All right, Pop, since you feel that way about it. But I'm beginning to think that coat will have to be platinum mink."

CHAPTER 6

"Do LET me take a peep," said Wendy as she approached Francie's sketchbook. The art class was out of doors for the first time that season, trying their hands at a scene with oak trees. The girls who attended this class were allowed an unusual amount of freedom; they talked at their work as the spirit moved them, and Miss Delvaux came to see them only once in a while, to offer her criticisms and suggestions. It made a very pleasant break in the day, an hour of quiet freedom and congenial work, for Art was not compulsory. For Francie it was an hour of pleasure. For the first time since she'd arrived in England, she felt like painting again.

"You're not too bad at this sort of thing, are you, young Nelson?" continued Wendy, inspecting the paper, and Francie felt appropriately gratified. It was silly to be susceptible to childish approval, she knew, but such things are contagious, and Wendy was an amiable character, generally respected by the other girls. She and Jennifer were prefects by virtue of seniority, though it was hard to think of seniority when one looked at her earnest young face with its snub nose.

"Let *me* see," cried Marcie Smythe. "I say, Francie, that's not bad. Not bad at all!"

"I don't honestly see how you do it," said Wendy, squinting earnestly at the water color. "I'd know that tree anywhere."

Francie said, "Oh, it's not good. Not really. I'd like a chance to do a big thing one of these days—something with the sea in it, or a great sweeping hill. All of this scenery is pretty, but too enclosed. Now if only we were allowed to keep cars we could drive over to the coast."

"Cars? D'you mean the girls owning them themselves?" Marcie gasped. "But nobody would ever be allowed to drive one. Aside from the shortage of petrol."

"Why not? A lot of the kids at Jefferson had their own. One boy I know has been driving since he was fourteen, and I've got a driving license myself. They let you take out a license at fourteen in my state."

"Oh, that. But owning a car at school——" began one girl.

Wendy and Marcie exchanged a glance, and Francie saw it. For a moment the incredulity she read in their eyes made her furious, but she remembered Pop's words just before she said anything she might regret. "It would be the same for you girls over here," she added quickly, "if it wasn't for the petrol rationing. I quite realize that."

"Really, do you think so?" asked Wendy doubtfully. "Somehow I can't see Mummy letting me drive or own a car however much petrol we could get. Perhaps my bro—but he's a bit older of course, and he'd never let me go along on a joy ride. Do you mean to say you could go out with that boy in his car, any time you liked?"

"Why, of course. All of us at school——"

"I forgot; your schools are coeducational, of course." Wendy hesitated, her forehead puckered. "I just can't imagine it," she said frankly. "Don't the students hate it? Mixed games might be fun for the girls, of course, but at most boys' schools here they simply hate it when they've got to arrange matches with us. I can imagine what my bro would say if you asked him to take out a lot of girls in a car. It wouldn't bear repeating, I'm sure. And what most of them think of coeducational schools. . . ." She paused, her voice expressing an extreme she could not put into words.

Francie painted silently for a little, busy with her thoughts. "Do all English schoolboys hate girls?" she asked at last.

"Oh, not really, I suppose—not *all* of them, *all* the time. But mostly they do, yes."

"In the States we get over all that nonsense by the time we're fifteen or so," said Francie. "It's just adolescent hostility. We outgrow it."

"Do you? We don't."

"No doubt," said Francie to herself, "but then you're all mentally retarded. Babies, that's all—just babies." Most of her classmates were nice, she was willing to admit that, but it made her want to laugh when she heard them talking about playing their best for old Fairfields, as if they were all football coaches. They were always saying things she had thought were only to be found in children's books.

Francie was becoming firmly convinced that they were ten years late growing up, at least ten. On several occasions when mothers and fathers came to visit the school Francie had been invited to join the family party when it went out to tea in the village. She had spent a few hours with Mrs. Tennison and Jennifer like that, and on another afternoon she went along with Wendy when Colonel and Mrs. Hardcastle came by to see their daughter and give her a treat. Both of these experiences left Francie feeling lost and puzzled. It was one thing she didn't feel like talking over with Penelope, who behaved just like the others. The girls had been so respectful, so childish! It was, "Thank you ever so much, Mummy," and "Dear old Daddy," and they maintained a generally sweet, subservient attitude that Francie simply could not understand. She remembered the cavalier treatment of parents that all her gang at Jefferson meted out. She seemed to have stepped onto a new planet.

"When do girls grow up in this country?" she wondered. Among her short-skirted classmates she felt more than ever like a wise old woman.

FRANCIE

Summer vacation was casting its shadow before, and at home the Jefferson gang began to make their plans early. One day Francie received letters which she flew to answer.

"*Dear Glenn:* That's wonderful! I'll be waiting at the station with a brass band. If you've got room in your bags, you might bring along Nellie Lutcher's latest records which Ruth writes are . . ."

"*Dear Ruth:* You were right; I got a letter this morning from Glenn and he and Bob Chapman are coming over about the first of July. They're going on to Paris and Norway, he says, but if I've got any influence they'll put off Paris, and I think I have. (That's a gag.) What gives, though, with Gretta?

"The brushes and paints and record album just arrived. Thanks for taking all the trouble. Now the only thing I need is a phonograph! Pop says he'll give me a little portable radio and phonograph for my birthday, and if I can promote him for it in advance I'll be all set.

"I'm sneaking time out to write this; the girls are all swotting for end-of-term exams. We get *three* sets of exams every year in England; this counts as second term and after the spring hols we go on for a third one, to the end of July. How do you like *that?* I hate it. But as long as I'm here I don't want to look like too much of a dope, so I'm working hard.

"You simply can't imagine this place. Not in your wildest dreams. These girls are morons emotionally, but really. In hall, where we eat, we move around from table to table, every week, so every girl sits at every table with every mistress at least once. The big moment, I should add, comes when it's your turn to sit next to the headmistress! And you can believe me or not, but they take it awfully hard. You and I have had our moments when we were very young, Ruth; there was the time you got Cary Grant's autograph, for instance, and I guess that compares to the day I thought Joe di Maggio looked at me. Well, Grant and di Maggio are as nothing compared with Cressy, that's the games mistress here at Fairfields. For a kind word from Cressy, girls allegedly our age are prepared to throw themselves off the Cliffs of Dover.

"Pop says we've got to visit the Tennisons during the hols. You can just picture my delight at the idea of spending a week with Jennifer, but if I don't it makes it awkward for him at the office, he says.

"It'll be nice to see Glenn, but it's not quite enough. I'm counting the days until we start home. . . ."

Francie paused and nibbled at her pen. She had written the usual phrase, but something about her surroundings, perhaps the shrill sound of a bird in a tree near the kitchen garden, made her stop to think. Was she really counting the days?

She stood up and moved over to the window. It was a morning from the advance pages of the calendar, a summer day handed to England on a plate, as sometimes happens. The grass, which to be fair to it had been green all winter, looked suddenly fresher, as if new juice were pushing up from the roots. The sun was shining, actually shining; it didn't glare, but it was there in the sky smiling down on Fairfields. The trees were still stark and bare, but Francie knew that in the thicket behind the stables there were dozens and dozens of snowdrops sweetly blooming. And in the air was a soft smell of something she could not put a name to, yet it was something she felt she had known far away and long ago; it brought an echo of some happy time all but forgotten.

No, she said to herself; I am not counting the days before I can get back to Jefferson. I'm not counting anything. She went back to her letter and crossed out the sentence.

The Tennisons lived in Surrey, about an hour's train ride from London. Even though it was only Jennifer's house they were going to, Francie felt pleased and excited as they set out from Pop's hotel. Four days of London, though with theaters and picture galleries and shopping expeditions, had not been really enjoyable. She felt lost in the great gray city; she missed the sparkling newness of the shops and restaurants at home.

"It's terribly cute at first," she explained to Pop, "with these poky little windows and all the stone buildings, but there's nothing for a girl to do, once I've been to the newsreel theater. I haven't got anyone to date, and I've got sort of used to being busy at school, I guess. I'm used to being regimented. At Fairfields every minute's accounted for, so that I'm always wishing I had more time to draw or paint."

"I hope they're not overworking you." Pop studied her. "No, you look fine," he decided. "I don't know when I've seen your cheeks so pink. Is it genuine?"

"Part genuine, but I'm afraid my hand's lost its old cunning with lipstick," said Francie. She had got out of the habit of putting on lipstick, because of course makeup was anathema at Fairfields. "It's so nice to wear regular clothes again," she said, settling happily into her train seat, in the corner. Pop grunted sympathetically as she gave herself an approving pat. She was wearing a new suit Aunt Norah had bought in Florida because, as she wrote, she couldn't resist it, it looked so much like Francie. It was navy, with a blouse and other touches of bright red plaid.

"There's Jennifer," announced Francie, peering through the window as the train pulled into their station. "There, the girl over there by Mrs. Tennison. See?"

"That little girl?" asked Pop in surprise.

"*Little?* She's a month older than I am! You never can tell, though, over here, can you? They look the same until they're married."

"Oh good," said Jennifer, greeting them more pleasantly than Francie had expected. "You've brought your racket, I'm glad to see. Isn't this spiffing weather?" Her eyes slid over the new costume and it seemed to Francie that their pupils narrowed vertically, like those of a cat. Jennifer still wore her school tunic, and Pop's mistake had been quite natural.

"*So* good of you to come this frightfully long way," Mrs. Tennison was saying. "Did you have a pleasant trip? No luggage in the van? Then perhaps we can go straight along to our poor old car—lunch won't wait very long, I'm afraid. And how was it in London? Wet? The girls will want to sit together, I suppose. Hop in, girls."

Chatting brightly about the weather in all its permutations she stowed the bags away, with Mr. Nelson feebly trying to help. It wasn't exactly a poor old car, reflected Francie, it was just an unfamiliar shape to an American, high and steep for its wheel base. They rolled off, down the village street between a few shops and then cottages.

"I hope you won't find those parcels too knobby, Frances," called Jennifer's mother over her shoulder. "One does one's marketing whenever one finds the opportunity."

"And the petrol," added Jennifer.

Francie felt shy and tongue-tied. Jennifer made no effort to break the silence between them, nor did her mother seem to expect any speech from the young people. Mrs. Tennison's was the only voice heard between the station and the house, and this seemed to be the normal state of affairs in the family. About a mile from the station the car turned into a cheerful hedge-lined driveway and drew up before a chubby-looking gray stone house with a tennis court. A Skye terrier rushed out at them from the door, yapping shrilly. The Tennisons said, "Be quiet, Bonzo! Bonzo! Bonzo! Quiet!" several times with no appreciable effect. They unloaded the car of parcels and baskets, as well as the Nelson luggage, to the noise of his yapping.

"We can manage *perfectly* well," said Mrs. Tennison in her bell-like tones. "No, really, Mr. Nelson, we can manage beautifully . . . It's awfully good of you. Just put them down on the table, if you don't mind. Coo-ee, Robert? Robert, are you there? We've arrived, darling."

They lived very comfortably, Francie reflected in surprise. It was her first experience of an English home, and she had expected to find a smaller edition of Fairfields, like a public institution in miniature. Hadn't everyone at home warned her? She was relieved, yet felt she had strayed into the wrong book, or onto the wrong stage.

The room they gave her was cheerful, with shabby chintz curtains at the large windows and a huge old-fashioned wardrobe. The whole house had a pleasant, lived-in look, she decided, thinking of the dining room where she had just lunched. There, all the family china seemed to be on display, plates propped on the molding against the wall, and cups and saucers in a glass-fronted cabinet. There was a lot of silver around, too; teapots and jugs and saltcellars and things, out in the open all the time. Bread sat on the breadboard, and cheese under a cover on the sideboard, with jam in pots. Francie thought of Aunt Norah's house where the mechanics of eating were so carefully hidden away between meals. Yet after all, why should they be? They weren't shameful symbols after dinner, any more than when the family was eating.

Jennifer and Francie did the washing up after lunch, getting their hot water from a terrifying copper tank which Jennifer called a "geezer" but which was spelled "geyser." Jennifer lit gas under it, at a jet that popped and spit, and then the water came down quite hot. "It's so much better since the Mater had this geezer put in," she said to Francie, who was watching in frightened awe. "We're on the town main now and all this is wonderfully simple. After our old boiler system for hot water, it's heaven. That *never* worked."

It wasn't exactly Francie's idea of heaven, but she had no intention of discussing such matters with Jennifer this early in the visit. Several months before she would have been unwise enough to describe Aunt Norah's plumbing, not as a boast but simply in a comparative spirit. She knew better now. The English were touchy. They were apt to take any mere statement of fact as a hidden insult. At any rate, Jennifer was.

Back in her bedroom Francie took the spread off the bed, folded it carefully, put on woolen bed-socks, and climbed under the quilt. Mrs. Tennison had suggested that she take a little rest, and this was by far the warmest place for it. The house *was* comfortable in most ways, but it was cold, though the Tennisons didn't think so. They had exclaimed all through lunch about the warmth of the day; it was all Francie could do to avoid her father's eye, though by this time the Nelsons were getting accustomed to hearing how warm the weather was, in spite of all the evidence.

Jennifer felt no need for a little rest, since she had not gone to the tremendous effort of making an hour's journey by train. Francie giggled as she thought of it; Mrs. Tennison was certainly awfully kind, but she had some odd ideas about young girls. She had sent Jennifer on an errand on her bicycle, to a neighbor's house. "In the country I feel no hesitation about letting her go alone," she explained to Pop, as if an apology was in order. "Of course, London's a different matter entirely; I never permit Jennifer to wander about alone in London. I'm sure you feel the same about Frances."

Pop had looked simply staggered. "She's got to have a chaperone, you mean?" he asked.

"Oh no. I'm not all that old-fashioned!" Mrs. Tennison laughed. "No, it's quite sufficient, to my mind, if Jennifer's accompanied by some young friend whenever she goes out. I'd feel no qualms about letting her go with Frances, for instance, the two girls alone. No qualms at all."

"Girls are so independent nowadays," added Jennifer's father. "A good thing too, in my estimation. Our parents overdid the coddling act, I always think."

"Of course they did," said Mrs. Tennison. "But this part of the country's perfectly safe," she said emphatically to Pop. As if she feared that she had frightened him. "*Per*fectly safe."

"How do you feel about tennis?" asked Jennifer, putting her head in Francie's door at three-thirty. "Just a game or two to warm up, before the others get here?"

"What others?" asked Francie drowsily. She had dropped off to sleep, after all, in the welcome warmth of the quilt.

"Mummy asked some people."

Imagine calling your mother "Mummy" at Jennifer's age, thought Francie. But a lot of the other girls at school did, as well as Jennifer. It was another proof of their incurable childishness, she decided. She replied with manufactured enthusiasm, "Sa-well! Meet you on the court in two minutes."

If Jennifer can be decent so can I, she said to herself as she tied her tennis-shoe laces. But the fact was, she didn't look forward to playing Jennifer, who was school champion. Tennis hadn't ever been Francie's best game; she wasn't bad at it, but she wasn't terribly good either. However, one must be a good sport, she reminded herself as she ran downstairs to the court, where Jennifer was tightening the net.

"Wizard court!" she said in surprised pleasure, jumping on it. "How lucky you are to have it right here."

Jennifer was gratified. "It's not just luck; Daddy and Mummy are frightfully keen as well as me," she said. "They keep it in shape and we're giving tennis parties all the time. We'll have to get your father out for a game or two."

"Oh, Pop won't play tennis," said Francie, swinging her racket. "He only fishes, and goes in for workouts in the gym in New York when he thinks he's putting on weight."

"How odd. Typically American." Jennifer's tone had taken on the old school tinge, that familiar, unpleasant intonation. I've done it again, thought Francie; just talking about New York must have done it. "Which side do you want?" Jennifer asked, changing the subject, and so they started the game.

It's never much fun playing somebody who is bound to win, unless your opponent plays with good humor. Jennifer didn't. The devil was in her; first she made Francie run all over the court, and when she tired of that she pretended she couldn't be bothered to play a decent game. She could beat Francie, she implied silently, with a hand and a foot tied behind her back. Demonstrating this, she grew careless and nearly lost a game. Then all of a sudden she snapped out of it and began playing sensibly. Francie guessed one of the parents had come out of the house to watch, but her back was to the door and she couldn't look around.

However, Jennifer's good behavior didn't hold up. She began sending over her serves with vicious force. Francie missed. Once, twice, once, twice——

"Hold on, there," called a protesting voice she didn't recognize. "What *is* this? A private fight?"

Two strange young men in light trousers stood beyond the wire, laughing at them. One was tall, dark, and thin, and the other was medium-sized and very fair—he was rather cute, Francie decided. They were both nice but he was the cuter. "It's war," she replied pertly, "but Jennifer attacked without any declaration."

"D'you want the court?" demanded Jennifer of the youth who had spoken, preparing to walk off. "I've got to give Mummy a hand now, anyway."

"Do take it," urged Francie as the young men hesitated. "I couldn't possibly play any more, not till I've puffed a bit."

Without more ado they accepted. She saw them hard at it as she carried tea cloth and plates in Jennifer's footsteps, out to the table on the lawn. They had completely dismissed the girls from their minds, she was interested to observe. For a moment when they first talked to her she thought she had seen a gleam of admiration in their eyes, especially in those of the blond boy, but she must have been mistaken. Never in her life, at any rate in her adolescent life, had she met boys who behaved like that, who didn't seem to care a bit whether or not she was there.

Nobody seemed to think of making introductions, but from a conversation she deliberately overheard between Pop and Mrs. Tennison, sitting on the lawn, she learned that the boys were named Peter and Mark, that Peter lived in the village where Mark, his friend (the cute one) was visiting him, and that both of them were constantly dropping in here to play tennis. Pop said casually how nice it was for Jennifer to have other young people around, an innocent remark that surprised and amused Mrs. Tennison.

"Oh, they've no time for *Jennifer*, Mr. Nelson! They're far too grand for such an unimportant little girl. They're grown up, you know—quite young men. They were both called up for the last year of the war, and now they're at Oxford."

"No time for girls, eh?" Pop's eyes twinkled.

"I don't know about that, but certainly they've no time for children like our chicks, who are still in the nursery. Or ought to be."

"I wouldn't say the nursery, exactly," said Francie's father. "After what I've seen going on among young folks, I doubt they're as indifferent as you seem to think."

Francie stole a glance at Jennifer as they carried plates of cake and sandwiches out to the tea table. Had she heard this exchange? Would she consider it in bad taste? But Jennifer's eyes were fixed on the sandwiches with what looked like genuine indifference to anything her elders might be saying.

"Shall I bring the brown sugar, Mummy?" she asked.

"No, my love, this will do nicely. You'd better go and tell the boys tea's ready."

From her stiff little chair near the teapot Francie watched the three crossing the lawn toward the table. The dark boy, Peter, idly reached out as he walked and tugged Jennifer's hair, whereupon she struck at him and he caught her fist and held it off. Then Mark pretended to trip her up. Both boys teased her as if she were a large baby or a good-natured pet dog, and like a baby or a dog Jennifer reacted to it, half-laughing, yet nearly angry. It was strange altogether, thought Francie. Nobody behaved like that in her crowd at home; in fact she couldn't remember indulging in any play in the same roughhouse spirit since she was twelve years old. Again she was astonished, as she so often was at Fairfields, by the simplicity of Young England's pleasures.

"Yet Jennifer's not quite as childish as she looks," she thought with a touch of spite. "She's liking it."

FRANCIE

Jennifer sat down next to her mother and began dispensing bread and butter like a little lady. Her healthy color was higher than usual, and as Mark swallowed sandwiches she kept glancing furtively at him. Evidently Francie was not the only one who thought he was cute.

An instinct stirred in Francie which had been long asleep. Ruth would have recognized the danger signals in her eyes. Francie Nelson was on the warpath.

"If you want to put yourself across with somebody," she had often said to Ruth, during long cozy chats in Jefferson over double chocolate malteds, "you've got to *mean* it. Be aware of the man. Concentrate. I can't tell you how to do it, exactly, but it works."

Now Francie concentrated on Mark. She worked hard at it, without showing any effort. All afternoon she stalked him like an accomplished hunter; she watched him, laughed when he spoke, dropped her eyes if he happened to look at her, and then when he looked again met his gaze squarely. She would have described the process to Ruth as "Treatment A." The first task, she knew, was to get past that ghastly indifference he seemed to wear like a coat of mail.

"I've done it," she thought at last, with a thrill of satisfaction.

She had done it, as a matter of fact, too thoroughly. Not only Mark but Peter as well suddenly began to pay her attention. And as a special triumph, it wasn't the rather contemptuous attention they bestowed on Jennifer. Neither of them tweaked Francie's hair or took other liberties of that sort. Instead they talked to her as to an equal. They asked her if she had visited Oxford. They requested her opinion on the latest movie showing in London.

It was a true victory, not the less so because it was invisible to the older people. Neither Mr. Tennison nor Mr. Nelson seemed to notice anything wrong. Pop was used to his daughter exerting influence over young men, whereas Mr. Tennison never took the slightest interest in what the younger generation did. Mrs. Tennison was determined to consider the younger generation humorous, and only humorous, in any manifestation whatever; she merely laughed at whatever Mark or Peter said, without listening.

As for Jennifer, her thoughts, if any, were her own. Her expression didn't change. After the tea things had been piled on a tray and carried indoors, with the young men eagerly helping, she said abruptly, "Well, come on. Who's for tennis?"

Nobody replied. Francie dropped her eyes and the boys waited. Mrs. Tennison said at last, "You children needn't hold back on our account. We can play later."

Still there was a pause. Francie said, "I don't believe I'll play, Jennifer. It's not a bit of good; I'm not up to your standard."

"Nonsense," said Jennifer. "You play perfectly well for a social game. Come on, let's have mixed doubles."

"No, really, I'm not good enough. Go ahead, the rest of you, and I'll watch."

"But——" Jennifer began.

"Go on, Peter; you can play Jenny. I've really had enough for the afternoon," said Mark. "Too much tea, that's my trouble."

In the end, it was Jennifer's parents who played.

Francie had expected to savor to the last drop her cup of triumph, but somehow it didn't work out that way. Jennifer showed no signs of dismay or disgruntlement. She continued behaving just as she had done before, dry, abrupt, and distant.

"I thought she'd seem younger and less of a threat," thought Francie ruefully, "but she doesn't. She can still get me down, just the same as always."

Francie even felt forced to respect her enemy, on a day when Mrs. Tennison's firm good humor failed her, and she had to go to bed with a sudden attack of arthritis.

"It's most inconvenient, I know," Francie heard her saying to Jennifer from her pillow, "but the grim fact is I can't straighten my back out, poppet. It *is* inconvenient, today of all days, because there's the joint to prepare and I had meant to do you a gooseberry tart. I know these attacks. I'll be better tomorrow, but for the afternoon I'm afraid you'll have to carry on without me."

"That's quite all right, Mummy," said Jennifer. "I have Francie, and we'll manage."

Her competent voice surprised Francie. "She must be mad," she thought. "How can she manage a joint and a tart? I know I couldn't, anyway."

But Jennifer did manage. She quietly took over the kitchen and proceeded to give a very good imitation of her mother. She prepared the joint, gave her orders to Francie with pleasant efficiency, cycled—accompanied by her respectful guest—into town to the baker's for a forgotten order of tea cake, and behaved in general as if housekeeping was the one thing she had always been trained to do.

"I do think you're a marvel, Jennifer," Francie burst out as they prepared a tea tray for the invalid. "I'm perfectly certain I couldn't do all this, I can tell you that much."

"Do all what?" asked Jennifer in honest surprise. "You mean the cooking? But I thought American girls were good cooks."

"Some may be, but I've never picked it up myself. My aunt did all that. And you seem to know exactly how to go about it."

"Cooking's something we've had to do all these years since the war began," said Jennifer casually, mixing the piecrust. "There wasn't anyone to help out, you see. It was different before; the Mater had to learn late in life. She'll tell you herself, she couldn't boil an egg before the war, but as it was she had to learn, and so did I—we struggled through together, as it were. We had to get down to it, I can tell you, when all the domestic help went into the factories. It's just as well I did." Her voice was cheerful. "I don't see any signs that we'll ever get more help, as things are going, but I don't mind cooking. I rather like it, as a matter of fact. If every study at school were as easily picked up, I'd be all right!"

Francie looked at her in wonder. Jennifer did not seem ill-pleased by the compliment, but she was confused, and broke off in relief when the little dog limped into the kitchen and gave her an excuse to change the subject.

"Bonzo, whatever is the matter with your paw? Let me look at it," she said. She knelt down and picked up the dog's foot. "Oh, the poor beastie!" she cried. "Look at this, Francie; his poor claw is simply mangled. He must have cut it, or got caught in a snare."

Francie tried to look, but a familiar weakness assailed her. "I'm awfully sorry, Jennifer, honestly, but I can't bear the sight of blood. I get nauseated. Do you mind if I don't come close?"

"No, of course, not at all, but you might fetch the surgical gauze from the cabinet over the bath —that is if your legs haven't given way."

Francie bit her lip. She had told the truth; she had always been silly about blood, but there was no help for it. Under the lash of Jennifer's scorn she meekly fetched and carried, while the English girl, still showing a surprising capability that Francie

FRANCIE

had never suspected, washed and bandaged the dog's paw midst a resentful silence. Hostility reigned again.

"Yet for a while there," reflected Francie, "she was quite decent. I must admit she *is* a good housekeeper. Just like a grown woman, really. Maybe these kids aren't as babyish as I thought."

Lately Francie had found no time to write her customary long letter to Ruth. It wasn't that the days were crowded with dates; to her disgusted surprise Mark didn't ask for a date at all, though she had fully expected him to do so when he took his leave after the tennis party. He had merely lingered a little saying good-bye, as if he wanted to do something about the matter but didn't quite know what. Now if he'd lived in Jefferson, thought Francie, he'd merely have said, "Are you busy Saturday night?" or at least, "I'll give you a ring in the morning."

Maybe he was afraid of the Tennisons. But what was wrong about dating? She never thought about the fact that dates are costly. American boys always managed.

So, unfortunately, it wasn't Mark or Peter who was keeping her busy; it was the weather. This remained determinedly fine, so that when she and Jennifer weren't cycling into town on errands for the household, or helping Mrs. Tennison with the cooking like good little girls, they were expected to be out of doors. They played tennis—Jennifer displayed better manners nowadays on the court, observed Francie, or perhaps her own game was really improving—and they went on picnics or walks, *en famille*. The Tennisons were determined to do their duty as hosts, and to show off the English countryside. Ordinarily they had to be very careful with their rationed petrol, but Mr. Tennison had saved some up for the occasion and on one day they even drove a long way out for picnic tea in a little wood. Not once, however, did they go to the movies.

As long as it was only for a few days, Francie told herself she didn't mind. But it would have been much better if Mark or even Peter had been along on the walks and the picnic. She wondered if she could have been mistaken, too confident, too conceited. Perhaps Mark hadn't really noticed her at all, she thought. These months in the strange country of England had made Francie begin to look at herself from the outside, wondering a little what the other girls at school thought of her. In Jefferson it had never occurred to her to wonder; they all felt the same way about things. But here——

"They'd think I was bats if they knew how often I think about Mark," she admitted to herself. "They're never keen on boys. Anyway, am I really keen on him? Or is it just that I like to have something going on?"

She pondered this difficult question, during the

long dull hours. It might even be, she felt, that Mark's only attraction was that Jennifer in her immature way liked him too.

On the fourth day in walked Mark himself, at last, carrying his tennis racket. After thinking about him so much Francie was surprised to see him. He wasn't quite so attractive as she had thought. Or was he?

She and Jennifer took turns playing him or each other, but it was a dull day and before tea it began to rain. The girls had to give him tea by themselves, for Pop and Mr. Tennison had gone up to town on a business matter and Mrs. Tennison was out interviewing a new charlady. Poor Mrs. Tennison, thought Francie, always working, standing in line to buy fish, or trying to locate a good dressmaker to alter her old clothes, or hunting high and low for curtain material. Aunt Norah never had to put in half so much time on her house. And with all Jennifer's mother's work, the food wasn't easy to manage anyway. Having to be careful with sugar, having to plan so many meals without meat—really, "the Mater" was wonderful. Francie, happy that Mark had come to tea, began feeling very kindly toward the Tennison family.

At last Jennifer muttered something about getting hot water and went into the kitchen. Francie was just thinking that it was significant how Jennifer had given up the school uniform, and blossomed out in regular frocks, when Mark said, hastily, "You know, Peter's most awfully smitten with you."

"Is he?" Francie felt slightly astonished. After all, it was Mark she had put in all that work on—not Peter.

"Yes. Awfully." He turned bright red with the effort of making such a personal remark. "I've never seen old Peter so smitten. He never looks at girls, in the ordinary way. It must be your being American. You American girls *are* different, you know."

"I guess we must be," said Francie. "Well, I mean, it's only natural in a way. We're brought up so differently."

"So I should imagine," said Mark. "English girls are jolly, of course, and all that, but you're—well, different. I don't know if you understand what I mean. The point I'm trying to make is, do you think your father might bring you to Oxford one of these days? Americans tend rather to like Oxford, I've noticed."

"Well, I don't know. Pop's usually busy, and——"

"Peter would be most awfully bucked," he said. Then Jennifer came back.

It was still raining after they had cleared away the tea things, so they went into the library where the occasion seemed to call for something special, and Francie suddenly had an idea. "Shall we try out my new phonograph?" she asked. "I've brought some records I just got from the States."

FRANCIE

They cleared a place on the desk for the machine and put on one of the new records. The music blared out. Francie's foot tapped restlessly. "This one's spiffing, isn't it?" she said. She began to dance by herself, unself-consciously, as she was accustomed to do in Jefferson. Mark stared in admiration, Jennifer gaped in simple horror.

"And now the other side," cried Francie, happily. "You must have heard this one, Mark—'Baby, It's Cold Outside.' This is the best version yet. Just listen!"

She danced around the library, her eyes shining. "Come on!" she cried.

Mark joined her, though he protested he had never tried this new style of dancing, which seemed more of an individual effort than one of partnership.

"Come, I'll teach you," cried Francie. He caught on quickly. Round and round the rather small room they went, alone, together, alone again, together again, and all the time Jennifer stared as if she didn't quite know what to make of it. In a few more minutes, Francie thought, Mark would be really good.

The library door opened, and there stood Jennifer's Mater and Francie's Pop. It occurred to Francie that Mrs. Tennison didn't seem at all pleased with the merry scene. Pop, though, waved cheerfully and said, "How you doing?"

Mark stopped dancing and looked guilty. "Oh,

hello, Mrs. Tennison," he said. "Francie's just showing me the latest from the States."

The record had come to an end as he talked, but Francie felt no impulse to put on another one. She was reminded somehow of that scene in the train with Miss West.

Mrs. Tennison sat down in the now silent room. "How is your mother, Mark?" she asked brightly.

Mark went home soon afterwards, and dinner with the Tennisons was a very quiet affair. Nobody was rude to Francie, nobody was stiff; as for Jennifer, she simply behaved as she always did at home, in a noncommittal manner. But something was very wrong.

"Now what have I done?" Francie asked Pop when they were alone.

"The Tennisons probably never hear that kind of music, and you'll have to admit it does take getting used to—I found it hard myself. And maybe they've never seen that kind of dancing. Never mind, honey, I know you didn't do anything wrong. We can't always please all the people all the time." He patted her shoulder. "Don't worry about it," he said.

That was all very well, but how, Francie asked herself when she was upstairs, could she stop worrying? It was a simply horrid feeling, and in somebody else's house, too—Jennifer's house, which made it much worse.

Pop had said—but Pop was only Pop; he didn't

really know what it was like. It was perfectly ghastly, to feel like this in somebody else's house, in somebody else's country.

After a few tears, Francie went to sleep.

CHAPTER 7

THE MORNING after they came back to London the Nelsons were quiet at their hotel breakfast. Pop was thinking, no doubt, about oil, but Francie brooded on the ill-starred holiday visit, and she was inclined to be listless and mopey. This time, she felt, it hadn't been her fault at all; hadn't Pop himself been on her side? He hadn't said a word about doing as the Romans do. Which meant that Mrs. Tennison was unjust, and Jennifer was a cat, and England was too difficult for words. Her American friends seemed far away. The only bright spot on the British map at the moment was Penelope, yet even at the thought of Penelope Francie did not cheer up. She felt worse, for Penny had written that she'd developed troubles of her own during the holiday.

Francie was not near to tears, but there was a small lump in her throat which threatened to become chronic. It was no use trying to eat. She was crumbling a piece of toast over her plate when Pop, who was reading a long letter, suddenly exclaimed, "If this isn't timely! Who do you think's here in England, not very far out of London? Your Aunt Laura!"

"Aunt Lolly?" Francie's face was transfigured. She dropped her toast. "Really, Pop? Oh, that's perfectly marvelous. Where is she? How come she's here?"

"Well now, let me figure it out," said Pop. "Martin's been stationed here, evidently, and Laura wrote to us about it some time ago. Your letter, or mine—I forget which—told her about our plans—it must have crossed hers and hasn't followed her back yet on a return trip. This letter's gone to Jefferson and then was sent here, as you can see by all the postmarks and addresses. The point is, she doesn't know we're over in England at all. She's been out at their rented place, The Warren, for the past six weeks, it looks like. Well, chicken, that's good news, isn't it?" He put the envelope on the table and smiled at her pleasure.

"What's Uncle Martin here for?"

"Advising the Government, as usual. He used to be on Unesco, and then they shifted him over to Uno, and now——"

"Never mind all that alphabet," said Francie, laughing. "It's enough for me that he's brought Aunt Lolly with him."

Laura Barclay was her godmother, called "aunt" by courtesy. She had been a school friend of Francie's mother, and through an adventurous busy life of traveling she had always kept in contact with her goddaughter, to the extent of visiting Jefferson whenever she came back to the States. Francie as a child had thought of her adored Aunt Lolly as a kind of fairy-tale person, and even now it seemed quite natural that she should pop up in England in this miraculous way.

"He'll be here," Pop was saying, "until the commission he's sitting on has finished the inquiry they're making, which is an unknown length of time, according to Laura, so she's taken this house out in the country. Why didn't they find somewhere to live in town, I wonder? It would be easier."

"Aunt Lolly hates living in cities," said Francie. "She always goes out into the country if she can possibly do it. Of course, it must be hard to get around in the country here, but——"

"Oh, they'd get an extra allowance of petrol," said Pop.

"What's the quickest way to get in touch with them?" Francie wondered aloud.

"Telephone," said Pop. "We can put a call through right now. That gives me an idea, honey. They're out in Hampshire and the house sounds big enough for any number of visitors, the way Laura writes, so why shouldn't you invite yourself out there for the rest of your Easter vacation? It would take a load off my mind. I'll have to admit

FRANCIE

I don't know how to keep you amused here in town."

"Of course, if she can have me. And you must promise to come out for the weekend. But—oh bother." Francie's face fell. "I can't, Pop, I was forgetting Penny. I invited her here to spend a few days. It's all fixed up with the hotel, too."

"But you could ask her if she minds waiting, couldn't you?"

"Ordinarily I could, and would," said Francie, "but I hate to do it just at this minute, because Penny's having a little trouble at home. With her stepfather."

"That's too bad," said Pop thoughtfully. "Anyway, we'd better phone Laura."

The hotel room when Francie returned to it looked ten times brighter than it had when she woke up that morning. Her grudge against England had vanished for the moment, and she felt like a different person as she put in a telephone call to the number on Aunt Lolly's letter paper. She wanted to jump with excitement and happiness when she heard Mrs. Barclay's voice and brisk accent.

"It's *me*, it's Francie!" she cried. "Yes, it *is*, honestly . . . No, I'm here in London. London! . . . I know, isn't it funny? I know you didn't . . . Can you believe it? Yes, Pop's here too. . . . Let him talk to you about it and explain, and then I'll come back."

It didn't take long for the compatriots to arrange a meeting as soon as possible. Aunt Lolly would not listen to any suggestion of delay; she swept the difficulty of Penelope out of the way in a trice.

"But of course you must bring her along, Francie darling. Why not? We've all the room in the world down here. *Of course!* I'm angry that you didn't think of it for yourself. Very well, pet, the two-thirty train this afternoon—Martin's working at home today so he can meet you—and you can arrange with your friend to follow when she likes."

"Oh, Americans *are* wonderful!" said Francie with a happy sigh as she hung up. "Just look how quickly that was all decided. The way they hem and haw over any arrangement at school would drive you crazy, Pop."

"You've got to remember that the English are more thorough than we are, Francie, and they do lots of things better than we can," Pop reminded her.

"I don't feel like making any allowances at all, just now," she said. "Do you mind? Wait a minute —I'm phoning Penny."

Here for the first time her high spirits met a check. Penelope was rather hesitant about changing plans.

"It's so sudden," she explained. "I don't know if Mummy will approve. I'll have to ask her."

"But why shouldn't you come? You were coming up to town anyway to be with me, weren't you?

And that was all right," said Francie. Inwardly, however, she was thinking, "Oh bother, now I've gone and been too impulsive again. These English, they never do anything sudden or a bit informal." She felt snubbed, and a little bit cross with Penny, though she knew it wasn't Penny's fault at all.

"It's not the same thing," Penny was explaining. "Mummy might say it's an imposition on your Aunt Laura, not knowing me . . . Now Francie, stop thinking I'm being stuffy. Yes you do, I can hear it in your voice."

Francie admitted it with a laugh. "If my aunt can fix it with your mother, though, you will come, won't you? That's all right then. I'd back Aunt Lolly against any book of etiquette in the world."

Back went the receiver on the hook, and up again, while Francie called Mrs. Barclay.

"Of course," said Aunt Laura. "That's to be expected . . . Naturally, Francie, no mother would send her daughter out into the blue without *some* . . . of course I will, you little goose. Nobody's been silly about this but you, yourself. I'll write to Penelope's mother this instant. No, I'll telephone her. I must say I like to see you busying yourself on somebody else's behalf for a change."

"She's such a good friend of mine, Aunt Lolly. I'd like a chance to find out what's bothering her— she's an awfully well-balanced girl usually, you see; it's not like her to worry. I'd be terribly glad to see you two together."

"All right, honey. We'll fix it," said Aunt Lolly cheerfully.

"Why do you live in a warren?" demanded Francie of Uncle Martin, who had met her at the station in an American roadster. The name of Aunt Lolly's place, The Warren, had puzzled her from the first.

"I wouldn't know," Uncle Martin said. "That's what they call the place, that's all. Laura took it sight unseen, after she'd written to a few agents, because they all told her it's so hard to find houses in England just now. She jumped at it. It's turned out pretty well, considering."

"Oo, I should just say it has!"

The Warren looked charming with its flat warm-red front between carefully clipped trees. It was a Queen Anne house, beautifully done up and furnished, with gleaming parquet floors. A white-capped maid opened the door. Aunt Laura was waiting to greet them, and Francie rushed to give her a big hug.

"And how's the English schoolgirl? Goodness, Francie, but you're simply enormous. Isn't she, Martin?"

"Big enough, but not enormous," said Uncle Martin, grinning. "She wouldn't thank you for that description. I'd say she's been a little cowed over here, haven't you, Francie?"

"Wait and see," Francie countered. "Aunt Lolly, is Penny——"

"Ye-es, Penny's coming," Mrs. Barclay broke in. "I *told* you it would be all right, didn't I? She'll be here in the morning. Now run along with Simmons and find out where your room is. Wash your face, and then we'll show you around."

Penny looked around appreciatively as Francie led her into the room they were to share. "Lovely!" she said. "Aren't we lucky! All this is exactly like a fairy tale."

"That's how Aunt Lolly has always made things seem to me," said Francie, "like a fairy godmother, when I was little. She was always the last word in posh and simply dazzled me when she would descend on our house in Jefferson, so well dressed and smelling delicious."

"She's charming," said Penny, "and the house is too. How clever of her to find it and to make it look so nice. It isn't really like a modern English house at all, is it?"

"No. It's more like Hollywood's idea of an English house . . . But Aunt Lolly hasn't done anything special to it, you know. I was asking her last night and she said it was this way when they got here. It's just little touches; she has a talent."

The girls sat in comfortable chairs at the fireplace, which in deference to Aunt Lolly's American ideas actually had a roaring fire in it, though this was a bedroom. The curtains were of quiet-patterned glazed chintz and the beds were four-posters, curtained in the same chintz.

FRANCIE

Penny sighed contentedly. "Such luxury," she murmured. "She's made the best of two worlds. I'm awfully glad you managed to get me here."

"That was Aunt Lolly," said Francie, laughing. "She can do most things. But your mother wasn't sticky about it at all, actually."

"No, as a matter of fact she wasn't." A shadow crossed Penny's face. "Poor Mummy. She was probably overjoyed to get me out of the house, so that the tension would relax a bit."

"Now then, just what *is* all this?" asked Francie.

Penelope found it rather difficult to state her grievance in a connected way, but in bits and pieces it came out at last. Her stepfather, she insisted, was a very nice man and exactly the sort of person her mother needed. It would be all right if there were no Penelope, but he had strong ideas about Penelope's future.

"Why? That's none of his business," said Francie indignantly, ready to fight for her friend.

"That's just the point; he thinks it is. You see, he's rather old-fashioned, and considers girls my age mere children. As Mummy's husband——"

"But you're practically grown up! Why, in a little while you'd be legally——"

"That's how I look at it, myself," said Penny, "but it's becoming fairly obvious that he and I simply don't agree on that. Which makes life awkward."

"It's ridiculous! In America——"

"We're in England," Penelope reminded her.

She went on to explain in detail. As she had told Francie on the boat coming over, she was passionately fond of the theater, and it was her ambition to make a career of it. Not as an actress, she often explained.

"There's not enough *in* acting," she explained earnestly, for the hundredth time. "An actress hangs about for months just to get some miserable little part that may last a few weeks, unless she's one in a thousand and is awfully lucky to boot. I don't merely want to show off on a stage. I want to *work* in the theater. What really does fascinate me, as you know, is producing and directing. There's plenty of room in the profession for a person who's willing to do the donkey-work, and that's exactly the kind of thing I love."

"Yes, of course," said Francie warmly. "Westers says you're really very good at that, too—at staging and interpreting. I'll bet you could get one of those scholarships in the Dramatic——"

"You *do* understand," said Penelope in relieved tones. "I don't know why I'm going in for all this woffle—telling you about it, over and over—but it does help me to collect my own thoughts. And I've been so squashed down these hols at home, Francie, you can't think! Uncle Jim won't let me talk about it at all. He keeps saying flatly that I'm not to train for the stage. He makes it sound as if I wanted to be one of those girls you read about, who die of hunger on the steps of the Theatre Royale! And he acts as if, now he's spoken, the whole thing is settled and done with. He's closed his mind absolutely to any sort of discussion. Of course I don't accept his attitude for a minute, but how can I drag poor Mummy into what would certainly be a family row?"

The girls looked at each other helplessly. "It's difficult, I can see that," admitted Francie, "but he can hardly interfere if your mind's made up."

"Not directly, but it's no help. And if he persuades Mummy to put me into a secretarial school——"

"Secretarial school?" Francie echoed.

"There's a day school near our village, where I'd learn how to type and do shorthand," said Penny. "They turn you out in a year. It's a very good place, I'm sure, but I'd never be able to go in for dramatic work from there. I'd lose so much time, too. It would be the end of me. Absolutely the end."

Francie was gravely worried. The thing she had always most admired in her friend Penelope was Penny's little air of being in full control of the situation, of being able to reflect calmly on her world. Now this self-possession of Penny's seemed to have dissolved. There were actually tears in her eyes. "She takes this terribly hard," Francie said to herself with a sense of awe. She realized that Penny's emotion was a stronger thing than she, or her friend Ruth for instance, had ever felt.

"You don't have to leave Fairfields yet, do you?" she asked in hushed tones.

FRANCIE

"Oh no, Uncle Jim's quite agreed to my finishing the year. But after that I'll either have to do as he says, or strike out for myself, and though I must say I like the idea in a way, it would be such a slap in the face for Mummy."

"Strike out for yourself?" asked Francie, awed.

"That is, go to London on my own and get a job," explained Penny.

"You mean absolutely on your own? Without any money?"

"Yes, why not? It's not hard to get jobs in London nowadays, that's one thing. I could be a salesgirl, I suppose, or a waitress in a teashop. But that wouldn't be getting me any nearer to the stage," said Penelope, "and it would be cruel as well, because Mummy would have to explain it away. It would cause any amount of talk in our village. It's forcing poor Mummy to take sides, and—oh, I do hope we won't have any unpleasantness! These things are so difficult."

"Your stepfather sounds awful," said Francie.

"No, he's all right. It's just his point of view. He's a strict disciplinarian."

Francie sniffed indignantly. "Strict, my eye! If it were me, I'd tell him where to get off."

"But Mummy——"

"Yes, I can see it wouldn't be as easy as all that," said Francie. "Oh dear. Well, let's try to put all of it aside for the moment and just enjoy ourselves. Aunt Lolly's got all sorts of plans and parties in her

147

head, and maybe by the time we go back to Fairfields I'll have had an inspiration, or you will, or somebody."

"We've spent a lot of time on my moans. Now tell me about yours," said Penny. "I shrieked over your letter about Jennifer and the glamorous young man. What happened after that?"

"Oh, nothing much. Nothing at all to tell the truth. We were rather quiet until it was time to come back to London, naturally. Poor Pop, it must have been a strain for him."

"Mind you, Francie, you *were* naughty."

"I expect I was," said Francie, sighing. "Everything I did seemed to be wrong, and after a while I didn't care. But never mind all that—it's childish compared with your troubles. Have you been thinking about the term play?"

Until tea they chattered with animation about this, their mutual interest. It had been decided by the faculty to play safe and put on *A Midsummer Night's Dream* at the end of the term.

"We always do," as Miss Maitland said, "and it's by far the most satisfactory arrangement. It's always the best school play. There are parts for the little ones, and there is plenty of scope for the older ones as well."

Penelope was to be the director and producer, and Francie's art class was to contribute all its talent to evolving the stage sets and scenery. Thus the friends had plenty to talk about; they were surprised when they heard the tea bell.

FRANCIE

Aunt Lolly had already made friends with her neighbors, and Francie soon discovered that The Warren, like all of Mrs. Barclay's places of residence, was open every evening to guests. There was a constant stream of people: Colonel and Mrs. Gresham from over the road; Mrs. Claye, the pretty widow who had the cottage just outside the village; Jock Bennett, a young friend Aunt Lolly invited in for the girls. There was in fact quite a scattering of girls and youths of their own age, home from school, like Francie, for the holidays. The ease, the familiar talk and interests, the knowledge that she was understood here and liked, felt as soothing to the American girl as a warm bath after exposure to cold rain.

"I wouldn't have guessed life in England could be so gay," said Francie as they changed for dinner. "It was so good to hear all the latest records from home! The Barclays are awfully lucky to have found a place with so many nice people living close by, aren't they?"

"Oh, I suppose you'd find just as nice people anywhere," said Penny sagely, "but they're slow usually in coming out of their shells. Your Aunt Lolly does something to people, I can see. She makes them nicer."

"They're playing bridge tonight, which is rather a nuisance," continued Francie, "though Pop will be glad, because he loves bridge."

"Why should it be a nuisance? You're not expected to play, are you?"

"N-no, of course not, unless I'm needed, and I never am. Aunt Lolly says I'll never make a good player. Only I was hoping we might have a bit of fun on our own."

"We can," Penny said. "They're playing in the library, and we younger ones can sing or play records or do what we like in the drawing room, I suppose. Why not?"

Francie was rather surprised by the question, but the more she thought of it the less she could reply. Why not, indeed? "I guess I take it for granted the older people ought to go out when I have a party," she confessed. "They always did in Jefferson."

"Never mind, Francie, you're in a good international house now, and you'll see how the other half lives!" Penny laughed as light-heartedly as if she hadn't an ambition or a stepfather in the world.

As Penny had predicted, the evening was a success and the generations managed to divide the house without difficulty. They went further; after the bridge-players tired of cards and when it was time for a nightcap they all gathered together in the drawing room and played games. If Aunt Lolly herself hadn't suggested it, Francie might have been scornful of the idea, but once they were embarked on "Twenty Questions" she admitted that it was fun.

One of the surprising things about the evening was Pop's behavior. From her limited experience of going to parties with her father, Francie had assumed that anything in company but bridge bored him. Tonight, however, he relinquished his game willingly when the time came, and joined the party very amiably. He chatted with Uncle Martin and Colonel Gresham, joked with the young people, and now and then watched Francie with an expression of approving relief. He too was enjoying himself, she realized. How pleasant and attractive he could be when he wasn't distracted by business! She was proud of him, glad that Penny could see him in this light, and glad, too, that he seemed easy in his mind about herself.

Pop went back to London on Tuesday morning. When he bade her good-bye he said, "Now be a good girl and take a real rest. I had a word with your Aunt Lolly about Penny's little difficulty. I don't know if Penny would like the idea of our hashing her troubles over, but in a pinch Laura Barclay's a sensible woman. It might help if Penny would talk to her."

"Thanks, Pop, I'll suggest it, anyway," said Francie gratefully.

Penelope didn't take the suggestion amiss, and that afternoon when the girls were at tea alone with Aunt Lolly they discussed the problem thoroughly.

"He does sound a difficult man," admitted Aunt Lolly, "but these things sometimes come out all right if one is patient. If I were you, Penny, I'd stop struggling just now. You're safe until the end of the next term, aren't you? Then if your Uncle Jim is still stubborn about the secretarial school——"

"Oh, he will be!" said Penny with a sigh.

"I'd leave it for the moment," said Aunt Lolly decisively, "and trust your mother to bring him round. When the time comes, if you *must* revolt, then you can gather your forces. But you ought to concentrate on schoolwork now."

Penny stared down at her plate, and Francie looked at her with sympathetic comprehension. She knew it wouldn't be easy for her friend, getting through the last few days of the vacation, living with her stepfather, without an explosion, but of course, what Aunt Lolly said was reasonable; it was no use stirring up the fight until the time came for it.

"Anyway, Mrs. Barclay," Penelope said, glancing up, "you *do* think I'm not entirely wrong? If a person knows and feels that she's cut out for one special kind of work——"

"Oh yes, I do agree," said Aunt Lolly firmly. "I think a young woman has a right to her own choice of work. I don't agree at all with your stepfather, as you describe him. But I don't know him, do I? I've no right to condemn his attitude until I've met him."

"No, of course not," said Penny.

"Then you *must* meet him," said Francie tempestuously. "We'll all meet him. On breaking-up day, so it won't look too planned, we can lure him into our group and turn Aunt Lolly loose. She'll set him to rights in no time. Oh dear, Aunt Lolly, I do wish we could get to work on him before then.

Are you absolutely sure you've got to go away next month?"

Laura Barclay laughed and said, "I'm no miracle-worker, Francie, though I'm touched and flattered by your trust. Yes, my dear, I'm afraid I do have to go. I promised a friend in Ireland I'd come over later in May, and that I'd stay at least six weeks."

"We'll have to postpone the reform of Uncle Jim, then," said Penny, "until you come back. I must say I agree with Francie, Mrs. Barclay; if anybody can bring him around you can. You have such a way with people!"

"It's a pity about Ireland," Francie went on, still lost in her thoughts. "This way, you'll probably miss seeing Glenn as well."

"And is Glenn so especially important?" asked Aunt Lolly. "Can't he wait?"

"Oh, he's not important in himself, I guess, but he's from home," said Francie. "I *am* awfully fond of him, and I'm crazy to see him and find out about everything in Jefferson. It will be heaven, really. . . ."

Aunt Lolly looked at her keenly. "Do you really hate Fairfields so much, then?"

Francie thought it over, while the others waited. "No," she said at last. "No, I don't. I have been dreading it a little, I admit, since we came here to The Warren. I've been wondering how I can bear to go back after this little bit of what I'm more used to. Actually it makes it easier, now there's been this break. It's wonderful your being here,

Aunt Lolly, but if I must tell the truth, Fairfields isn't so bad."

She knew she sounded confused, but Aunt Lolly seemed satisfied. They talked about Glenn's plans, and decided regretfully that there was no chance of bringing him to The Warren, as his visit would probably be over before Mrs. Barclay returned from Ireland. Then Uncle Martin came in and asked for coffee, and the talk turned to the general situation in England.

"I think they're on the upgrade," said Uncle Martin flatly. "I get sore at these people in my department who come here for a quick look around and then go home and talk to the papers about ruin and muddle."

"But do they really?" asked Francie.

"Oh yes. You don't see the papers at home, I suppose, except once in a while, but I can tell you it makes me pretty hot. They say the English won't work, the English are being lured to Communism, the English this, the English that——They've no idea of how sober and steady the English are. I've had some experience myself with rationing, for example, here and on the Continent and at home. Let me tell you, it *works* here. Yes sir, it *works*. These people still have principles. They know what's right and wrong. Do you realize what that means in the world today?"

"We do realize, Martin," Aunt Lolly said.

"I get carried away," said Uncle Martin, laughing. "You'd think I was making a speech in the Senate." He poured himself a cup of coffee.

Francie turned to the forgotten Penelope to say something. She paused and remained silent. Penny was looking at Uncle Martin, her face flushed and her eyes bright.

"Oh, I'm awfully glad he made that speech," said Francie to herself.

CHAPTER 8

"Back at Fairfields, May 15.
"Dear Ruth:

"I hate to think how long it's been since I had time to send you more than scrappy little notes, but as you must have guessed, my Easter vacation turned out to be busier than I expected. I hope you got our postcard from The Warren. We were feeling silly so we all signed it, Aunt Lolly and Uncle Martin as well as Penny. Oh dear, it was such fun, and how I did hate to come back here.

"Still, it could be a good deal worse. Honesty compels me to admit that Fairfields in May is a very different place from Fairfields in February. There hasn't been any rain since term began, touch wood, and that makes a welcome change to begin with. Whenever they decide it isn't absolutely freezing we hold class out of doors. We're in summer uniforms, too. (I still put on my long underwear under the cotton dress, but as I suspect that's cheating, I keep quiet about it.)

"I oughtn't to go on crabbing, because I do like school better now. Besides, I had a good long time to wear regular human clothes while I was in London and with Aunt Lolly. As a last beautiful gesture before I came back, Pop took me sightseeing up to Oxford, ostensibly to improve my soul and add to my culture, but actually I think because Mark and Peter wrote us a cute little formal invitation. It was a lot of fun. Not just what we might call fun if we were students at State, mind you; I can't imagine sightseeing in the same way with American boys. Mark must have gotten an exaggerated idea of my tastes because he found out I hang around art galleries a little in London. Anyway those boys walked us miles and miles through dozens of colleges and quads. I've seen enough old buildings and chapels to give me a passing grade in European History when I come home, without the trouble of studying at all. I learned to say University instead of College when I mean University, too. We wound up an improving tour with tea in Mark's rooms in College, properly chaperoned by Pop and a professor's wife. A lot of cute boys came in and made a fuss about—what? do you want to guess? Well, it wasn't me. Nobody paid much attention to me. It was the chocolate eclairs that Mark had ordered specially. They were the life of the party. The fact is, most boys here don't seem to like women at all. They treat them badly.

"On the whole, Ruth, I think you and I will have a better time at State. But Mark's attractive in his way, I must admit, and he isn't quite indifferent to the nearly Beauty Queen of Jefferson High.

"Have you seen Glenn lately? He still says he's coming over with his car, and it can't be long now. Oh, boy.

> "Yours, still going strong,
> Francie."

Penelope came back to school in a downcast frame of mind. In spite of Aunt Lolly's advice there had been more quarrels with Uncle Jim. "I did try," she said in woebegone tones, "but he started it himself, all about this being my last term. It makes me feel like a condemned criminal. I suppose I talked too much about the play—the *Dream*. It's been on my mind, naturally, and I spoke about it sometimes to Mummy and that must have irritated him."

"We can talk about it here as often as we like," said Francie comfortingly. She herself was becoming excited about the production, and with very good reason, for the girls in the art class, with one voice, had selected her as chief scene painter and designer. The responsibility of such a task thrilled and half-frightened her. She found herself chattering about it even to Miss Maitland herself, the first day she sat next to the awesome headmistress in Hall.

"To think I've been so worried all year about what I'd talk about to Miss Maitland," she said wonderingly to Penny later, as they went toward the tennis court. "It was as easy as anything, once we got started. I almost forgot it was *her*. I wouldn't have thought it possible!"

Marcie interrupted them with an eager inquiry: "Did you ask Miss Maitland about—you know, about giving the show out of doors?"

"Yes, I did," said Francie. This had been a much-discussed question among the young artists. The *Dream* when it was first produced, argued some of the literary students, was an out-of-doors play, or masque, acted among genuine trees under the genuine sky. This being so, it would be wrong to present it between the confining four walls of Hall, they claimed.

Francie naturally opposed this notion, for two good reasons. It was sure to rain, she said, if they counted on fine weather, and many of the other girls backed her up in that.

"It always rains on breaking-up days," they maintained when the fresh-air fiends waved almanacs at them, or cited the statistics of weather experts.

The other reason was obvious: if the play were to be presented in the oak wood, there would be no scene painting, or at best very little. Thus the work of the art class would be minimized. Opponents of the indoor school of thought were not slow to point this out, and to accuse the eager artists of prejudice.

"Yes, I did ask Miss Maitland," said Francie now, flushed with triumph. "She said it was far too much of a risk to count on an out-of-doors performance of any kind, ever! That is, a performance like this. On breaking-up day they always do P.T. shows outside, she said, and that sort of thing, because that can be called off without too much heartache, or moved indoors whenever you like."

"I knew all that, of course," said Jennifer loftily when Marcie scampered across to report to the other court. "We all know that, except newcomers like Francie. I should have thought even your precious play could be risked, myself. It didn't rain last year, if you remember."

"But we had the play indoors, anyhow," said Marcie. "We always do." Jennifer shrugged and turned her attention to the game.

"If she cared in the least for painting or stage work," said Wendy during one of the drama-class discussions, "Jennifer would be the keenest of the whole school on this play. As it is, she's not helpful. In fact, she's positively obstructive."

"I know," said Penny regretfully. "I'd find it much easier to round up the little girls, the fairies and all that, for rehearsal, if only Jennifer would set the example. As it is, she stirs them up to cut."

Francie listened as long as she could without contributing to the conversation. She knew that any criticism she might make of Jennifer would be attributed to the well-known enmity between them. At last, however, she could not resist; she broke in with a surprised exclamation.

"But if she keeps the little girls away," she said, "isn't that *sabotage?*"

"Of course it is, Francie," said Marcie. "That's just what we're saying."

"But can't we do something about it?"

Wendy Hardcastle said, "What do you suggest we do? We can hardly run and wail about it to Miss Maitland. The thing is, Jennifer has a tremendous following with the younger kids. And she's super with them, I must say; guiding and all that is Jennifer's *thing*."

"What's guiding?" asked Francie.

"My dear Nelson, what an ignorant barbarian you are!" said Wendy. "Guiding is working with the Girl Guides, of course, as group leader. Jennifer has a group of Guides in her village at home, and takes no end of trouble organizing them and looking after the Brownies—that's the baby ones—at their summer camp, and taking on all sorts of dreary jobs such as that. Do you mean to tell me there are no Girl Guides in America?"

"We call them Girl Scouts," said Francie. "I was a Brownie myself once, years ago."

"To give Jennifer her due," Wendy went on, "she's a really good influence on these horrid children, usually. Of course she oughtn't head them off our play, but . . . Being a prefect isn't my cup of tea, admittedly. I am one, but I don't enjoy it. Since we *have* to have prefects, it's just as well we've got a few Jennifers among us to do the job properly! Heaven help us, Francie, if the world's work had to be done by people like you and me!"

Everyone laughed, and Francie was left with something new to think about. She was impressed with the general fair-mindedness of her friends, which Wendy's opinion summed up. They didn't like a lot of things about Jennifer, but they gave her credit for the qualities they knew she possessed.

"Now if it were just me," Francie reflected, "I would decide to hate Jennifer through and through, forever. In fact, that's what I've already done. They don't go to extremes the way I do. That's a good thing." Besides, they took very seriously the quality of leadership. She could see that. Jennifer had a following among the younger fry, Jennifer was a good leader, and they cheerfully admitted it and respected her accordingly.

Francie could not quite scoff at the prefect system as she would have done when she first arrived. It had one advantage; it made the girls independent in many ways of their mistresses. They were not watched all the time, as she had expected they would be. They were free to set up their own world, within larger limits . . . After all, Fairfields was not a kindergarten, and it wasn't run like one. Mrs. Tennison, she recalled, had been far worse in her strictures than Miss Maitland was.

Aunt Lolly went off to Ireland, and Pop, too, suddenly departed, not for Ireland but the Near East. He wrote Francie a hastily dictated letter before he left, explaining that an emergency called him away but that if all was well he'd be back within the month. She ought to have felt forlorn and deserted under these circumstances, but life at school absorbed most of her thoughts and the world outside didn't seem to matter as much as it had before.

"After all, we're practically isolated for the whole term, until the end of July," as she said to Penelope, "so what's the difference where my people are?"

The fine weather deserted them for a fortnight and then came back. Trees put out buds and the early primroses and daffodils died off, giving way to a riot of flowers sweeter and more varied than Francie had ever seen in Jefferson. Then lilacs bloomed. The whole countryside was enchanting. If Glenn didn't arrive soon, Francie thought, he'd miss the best of it, but Penny laughed at her fears and said there would be flowers well on into August.

"You needn't be afraid everything will be burnt up by midsummer," she said. "This is chilly England. It almost never gets very hot here, you know."

"I've had to rearrange all my ideas of the seasons," confessed Francie. "You know, I used to think the poets were simply sappy when they talked so much about spring. Spring in Jefferson isn't so much, to tell you the truth—here today and gone tomorrow. My favorite season's always been the fall. Now, after seeing what spring can be like in

England, I'm beginning to understand the poets. The lambs and the rabbits and the fruit blossoms—oh, it's marvelous! And some new delicious smell practically every day. Except, of course, when they put bone fertilizer on the field," she added as an afterthought.

"You had better get over any ultra-dainty ideas like that," said Penny warningly, "before our cycling picnic. No one can guarantee that we won't go near bone fertilizer somewhere on the way. This is farming country, after all."

One of the weekend outings that the girls most looked forward to, as Francie had discovered, was the cycling picnic that the school took every summer when weather permitted. Now that the vexatious affair of her bicycle had been settled she felt inclined to share in the common excitement, but a few months before she would have hesitated to go out with the others.

The trouble had been typical of all her troubles at Fairfields. It began when Pop discovered that his daughter needed a bicycle at school. He had overlooked this requirement during the busy, hurried shopping days before she left London, and when he was reminded, a fortnight after Francie went to Fairfields, he hurried out remorsefully and bought one, and shipped it down to her immediately. Pop was an impulsive shopper. The task of buying most things bored him, as it does many another busy man; he would not look around before choosing; he was apt to order the most expensive article he could find, and assume that he was thus sure of getting the best.

There was no argument at school about the superiority of Francie's bicycle, as a matter of fact. One could see it at a glance. The difficulty lay in the fact that it was not the thing in Francie's circles to own a new bicycle. Girls at Fairfields School prided themselves rather on their shabby, beat-up machines; the worse-looking they were, the better. Wendy Hardcastle was admired and envied because hers had belonged to two elder sisters in turn before her advent at Fairfields. Thus poor Francie's magnificent chromium-glittering bicycle made her the butt of many merciless taunts, especially, of course, from Jennifer Tennison.

It was no use rebuking Pop for having been kind. There had been only one thing for Francie to do, in order to escape the annoyance of jeers whenever she went out on her bike. She set earnestly to work to rub off the pristine shine. Whenever she had a moment's privacy near the bicycle shed she sandpapered the enamel, hammered at the handle bars, scratched the leather saddle and even managed one whole weekend to leave the bike out in the bushes behind the school, where it was rained on for several hours. After that she did not feel conspicuous any more, and the girls let her alone on that topic. Even Jennifer forgot the original offense.

"Do you think the rain will hold off?" Francie asked now.

Penny said, "According to the BBC weather report it's going to be fine. In spite of that, though, it may not rain. In fact I'm sure it *will* be fine."

Together they solemnly inspected the sky. It looked hopeful; there were only a few harmless-looking cottony clouds in it. Satisfied, they started down to collect their machines and join the others.

"Only I do wish it wasn't Cressy in charge of our group," said Francie as they went.

"Why? Old Cressy's not a bad sort. I didn't know you didn't like her."

"I do like her all right, but some of the kids who have a pash always try to ride next to her when we're out on our wheels, and with so many of us today, we're apt to bunch a bit at the curves in the road."

"Ah yes," said Penny equably, "but they're not really silly with their pashes. Anyway it's not our affair to keep the crowd in order. It's up to the prefects to make us string out in proper formation on the high road."

"Thank goodness! I don't envy Tennison and Hardcastle that job today," said Francie.

The fourteen who made up their group set out at about eleven o'clock, all in order, with a picnic lunch divided into parcels which they carried in their handle-bar baskets. Each group was permitted to take its own way to the meeting ground where they were to lunch. Miss Cressall had already planned their route, which she knew from former years, with a careful eye on the necessity of avoiding much-frequented roads, and yet with the idea of taking a pretty, roundabout journey. Cycling in England, Francie had learned, was a common but dangerous form of exercise. No matter how careful their riders might be, bicycles were bound to wobble sometimes, and make little unexpected dashes toward the middle of the road. This wouldn't matter if all English roads were straight, but that was just what they were not; they curved and wandered between high banks or thick hedges. Constant watchfulness was necessary when the girls rode out for their picnic. Jennifer and Wendy did a sort of patrol duty along the fringes of the procession, except when the way led along a safe meadow path or through a wood.

They had been out for half an hour and were just coming out of such a comparative sanctuary onto a wide road which seemed deserted. Miss Cressall at the head held out her arm to indicate that they were supposed to turn sharp left. Then she blew her whistle sharply, and Francie, halfway back in the line, saw the reason. A big delivery truck—what the British call a van—came bowling around the corner which would have been ahead of them if they had all been riding on the road. Fortunately they were still in the pathway. It was just at the moment when most of the girls stopped pedaling and were stepping down to wait for further orders.

The van's driver had underestimated his speed. Like many people going around a corner he went wide, and drove over to the wrong side of the road before recovering. On a quiet highway such as this, he probably reasoned, it couldn't make much difference. Nor would it have mattered, except that Jane Mackay wasn't paying attention.

Jane was one of the younger girls and she had a notorious "pash" on Cressy. She was always hanging about the games mistress, working hard to play well on the team so that she would get a word of commendation. Today ever since the start of the expedition she had been riding her bicycle as close to the leader as possible, taking advantage of every opportunity to speak to her.

Like a sensible woman, Miss Cressall never took notice of Jane's fondness, though it must sometimes have bored her. Perhaps she felt that as long as Jane worked the harder because of it, it was as well left alone. Jane's contemporaries sometimes teased her, but Francie had long ago noticed that at Fairfields these emotional phases were usually ignored or taken for granted, which was after all the least painful way of dealing with them, especially as they never seemed to persist beyond a term's duration anyway.

Just before the wheeled cavalcade came to a halt, Jane had managed to think of another excuse to speak to Cressy. She turned her bicycle's front wheel out of line and speeded up, an easy task on the broad smooth pathway. Full of her own intentions she failed to see Cressy's commanding signal to pause, and for some reason ignored the whistle. When the others stopped, just as the van rocketed along toward them, Jane's bike went ahead full speed onto the road.

"Careful, Jane!" cried Miss Cressall, but it was too late to stop the girl.

With the quick eye and immediate reaction which the games mistress had developed during years of hockey and netball, she rode out between Jane and the oncoming menace. As if she were playing polo she "rode off" the other bicycle, forcing it into the shallow ditch that bordered the road. At the next moment she threw herself off her bicycle and as it clattered down, crushed beneath the van, she hurled herself across the ditch onto the grass beyond. A fencepost stopped her flight in midair. Miss Cressall fell to the ground and lay motionless.

For a moment there was wild confusion. The van came screeching to a stop some rods beyond them, and the driver climbed out and hurried back, looking angry. In the meantime the girls had crowded around Jane and the unconscious games mistress, all talking at once.

Jane struggled slowly to her feet, white and shaken. Her knees were grazed and bleeding; so was her cheek. Her particular friends seized on her and examined these wounds, but the others were all concentrated on Cressy, who didn't move. Shrill excited chatter filled the air.

"Don't you know better. . . ." the van driver was demanding in rough tones above the rest of the noise.

Francie, appalled, lingered outside the group, unwilling to add to the confusion though she longed to help. The younger girls, she could see, were utterly disorganized, and she didn't know what she should do about it. It was with relief that she saw Jennifer pushing her way into the middle of the crowd and heard her shouting, "Quiet, everybody!"

As usual, Jennifer's personality had an immediate effect on the smaller girls. Slowly the hubbub subsided.

"Move away from here," went on Jennifer. "Wendy, you see that they all stand back, will you? We must have room; Cressy won't be able to breathe."

The girls slowly shuffled apart until the games mistress lay completely exposed to Francie's view. Her face was half-turned toward the ground; her eyes were closed. She looked pale, but was breathing quite loudly. Jennifer knelt down and examined her in an efficient manner, not moving her more than to lift one arm.

"Here, miss," said the van driver more politely since his first excitement had ebbed, "let me give you a hand."

"What for?" asked Jennifer absently, her eyes bent to Cressy's face.

"We'd best put her into the van and get her to the hospital, hadn't we?"

"No," said Jennifer. "She mustn't be moved."

"Oh yes, miss," he said in shocked tones. "We ought to get her to hospital."

"No," said Jennifer, shaking her head. She stood up and looked over the crowd of frightened girls, and Francie, like the others, felt herself depending on this very young woman who seemed to know exactly what to do. Unwillingly, even now, the American girl felt admiration stir in her mind.

"One of you had better go with the van to telephone the nearest hospital and ask them to send a doctor," Jennifer said. "Who's got enough sense among you? Here, Penny, you go. Ask Enquiries what the nearest hospital is and get on to them. Tell them we haven't moved her for fear it's concussion; that she's breathing all right and as far as I can see there are no external injuries. Tell them her head hit the fencepost. It was an awful crack," she added, lapsing suddenly into her ordinary schoolgirl's voice. "I heard it; didn't you?"

There was a murmur of agreement. The van driver and Penny went off, and Jennifer said briskly, "Which of you was carrying the bottle of hot tea? Hand it over; we must put that at her feet."

"Shouldn't we make her a pillow out of a coat or something, Jennifer?" asked one girl. Jennifer said, "Definitely not. They taught us in First Aid never to move the patient's head unless it was absolutely necessary. We mustn't move her at all. But I nearly forgot one thing; we ought to keep her as warm as possible. Everybody give me your blazers."

In a moment Miss Cressall was warmly covered with blazers and sweaters. And that was all they could do, said Jennifer, until somebody older and wiser arrived to take charge. Now she turned her attention to the unfortunate Jane, and with Francie's help bound up her wounds.

"I thought you were afraid of blood," said Jennifer to Francie as they worked.

"I forgot all about that," admitted Francie. They were interrupted by a strangled sob from Jane.

"Do shut up, Jane," said Jennifer, wrapping a rather grubby handkerchief around the child's leg. "Whatever's the use of howling?"

"It was all my fault!" blubbered Jane.

"Well, what of it? Everybody knows you didn't do it on purpose, and it doesn't help to act like a baby now and set the other kids off." Jennifer's tone was kinder than her words, and Jane wailed,

"Oh, Jennifer, what if she's *dead*? I'll—I'll——"

"She's not dead, you idiot. I promise you that. Now blow your nose and keep quiet; we're too busy to keep an eye on you."

A few moments later the ambulance arrived, with the van close behind it.

"Cressy's suffering from slight concussion," Penny reported that evening to the dormitory. "I waited in the office because I heard them telephone about her, and afterwards Miss Maitland told me. Cressy ought to be back in a fortnight, as good as new. They said Jennifer did exactly the right thing from beginning to end. The doctor complimented Miss Maitland on her girls and she was awfully pleased; I could see it."

"Jennifer's a surprising girl," said Francie thoughtfully. She had been deep in thought all afternoon.

"Oh, Jennifer's a solid citizen all right," said Wendy. "You can always depend on her in that sort of crisis."

"Shhh," said Marcie, as Jennifer came in.

"Hello," said Jennifer. "I've been looking everywhere for you, Francie. I wanted to say you weren't half bad the way you kept young Jane quiet, coming back this afternoon. Very helpful it was; she was nearly in hysterics. Fancy a Yank being useful!"

The girls all laughed, Francie with the others. The compliment was so exactly like Jennifer!

CHAPTER 9

A FEW of the cast of characters were rehearsing privately out beyond the chapel, in the field. Small daisies starred the grass, but June had brought out a hundred other flowers which Francie could not remember ever having noticed in the States. At the moment she was glad to think about flowers because the rehearsal, as is customary with rehearsals, was boring. She had consented to take a very small part in the play because they were short of actors, but her heart was really in the other branch of stagecraft: scene designing and execution. Only Penelope, she reflected, could have persuaded her to take this on as well. Penny, in the absence of the advisory mistress, was in complete charge of the rehearsal today, and she had asked Francie to try to criticize the general effect.

"If I were to tell her the truth," thought Francie, "I'd have to say it's pretty stinking. But then a play always does stink at this stage."

Sheila playing Hermia, with Marcie as Lysander, was running through a love passage. Love passages as played at Fairfields were difficult to a degree that always, ultimately, made Penny tear her hair and declare wildly that she could not, would not go on. She was nearly at the hair-tearing stage right now.

Marcie gabbled:

" 'The course of true love never did run smooth
But either it was different in blood——' "

Francie gritted her teeth as she waited without hope for Hermia to interrupt. She knew it all by heart by this time, of course, and she knew as well that Hermia would not interrupt on her cue, because she never did. Sheila was a pretty little girl with pink cheeks and a most forgetful mind. At the moment her eyes were fixed dreamily on the summer sky and her mouth was open. She was a thousand miles away.

"Hermia!" barked Penny.

Sheila jumped. "Eh? Oh, sorry. Where were we?"

"You're supposed to interrupt here," said Penny wearily. "It's where you say, 'O cross!' "

"Oh yes. 'O cross! too high to be enthrall'd to low!' "

" 'Or else,' " said Lysander, " 'misgraffed in respect of years——' "

" 'O spite! too old to be engaged to young!' " Sheila, working up now to her favorite passage, did not again let her attention wander.

Lysander said, " 'Or else it stood upon the choice of friends——' "

FRANCIE

" 'O hell!' " began Hermia, and promptly broke down into helpless giggles. The other actors on the stage likewise broke into giggles. They invariably did at this speech. Even the sophisticated Francie giggled at the contagious silliness.

"It's no good," said Penelope with a dangerous restraint that they all recognized. "I've gone through this ridiculous business for the last time. I've warned you, and this is the end. With every single rehearsal you idiots get worse when we come to this point. It's not safe, so I'm simply going to cut out these speeches."

"I say, Pen, I'm awfully sorry," said Hermia, sobering.

Penny ignored her, and grimly marked her prompt-copy with a pencil. She looked up again at the sheepish crowd. "Ready with your next speech, Lysander," she said.

Francie ceased to listen. Out of the corner of her eye she had seen Jennifer wander onto the scene and an inspiration had come to her. Ever since the accident, she and Jennifer had been enjoying an armed truce. They didn't like each other any better, but a certain mutual respect had come into being between them.

"You know something, Tennison?" Francie said without preliminary greeting.

Jennifer waited, casting a superior eye over the scene Penny was struggling to direct.

"I've just been wondering," Francie went on

guilelessly. "I mean about the terrible morale among the younger girls in the play. You know—the fairies and what-not. You'd think nobody had ever taught them a bit of discipline. Do you suppose all this Girl Guide stuff you go in for does a bit of good?"

Jennifer stared. She knew perfectly well why the fairies were undisciplined: she'd filled them with her own considerable disrespect for the play. But this attack on the Girl Guides had caught her off guard.

Francie went on dreamily. "You'd think with the training you put them through they'd know how to do what they're told. But they haven't the faintest notion of how to follow directions. That's why I wonder if you're doing much of a job." She turned her back on Jennifer and moved to a place where she would have a better view of the players. Jennifer snorted under her breath and stalked off the field. It was the first time Francie could remember that *she* had had all the words, instead of Jennifer. She smiled wryly.

"My, but I'm a sly one!" she murmured to herself.

The weekend of half-term was marked by an incursion of parents, anxious-faced adults who made gigantic efforts to get to Fairfields for the day. For those girls whose fathers, or mothers, or both had taken this trouble it meant a day out on picnics or in expeditions to Farham and Kingston, the nearest towns, where one could eat strawberries at the local inns and visit the Museum.

Many Fairfields inmates found themselves at loose ends, as their parents had not been able to get there, owing to petrol shortage or other difficulties. These girls were, in fact, in the majority, as since the war it had become quite the normal thing to be left without family plans on half-term day. Francie had known for some time that she would be among their numbers, because Pop had found it impossible to get away from the Near East as quickly as he had hoped. Pop's business always took longer than he originally planned and Aunt Lolly, who might have come over otherwise, was still in Ireland. The American girl did not consider herself at all badly used, so it was with a sense of indignation as well as perplexity that she received a last-minute invitation from Mrs. Tennison, of all people.

"I'm so afraid you'll feel lonely on half-term day with your father away," wrote that lady. "Won't you come with Jennifer for a nice long walk with us next Saturday?"

"I just *can't*," said Francie as she showed the card to Penelope. "I don't want to spend the whole day with the Tennisons. How on earth can I get out of it politely?"

"I thought you and Jennifer had buried the hatchet," said Penny.

"We have, but that doesn't mean I love her mother any better than I did before. Jennifer's all right in her way, but I can't imagine being pals with Mrs. Tennison. Not in this world at any rate."

"Oh, well, it's simple enough; just say vaguely that you're awfully grateful and all that but you'd unfortunately made other plans before you realized and so forth. She won't check up; she's just trying to be kind. I don't suppose she really likes you much better than you like her."

"Loathes me, I should think," said Francie cheerfully. "I don't blame her for it either." She went off to write her note, and as it turned out she told the truth after all; with the next post she did have other plans made for her.

"Mummy's driving up," announced Penelope, bursting into the dormitory. "She's figured she can spare the petrol, and she's invited you to spend the day with us, lunch and all."

"How nice of her, Penny. I'll come like a shot, of course, if it's all right with you. Is your stepfather coming with her? I do hope so. I'm dying to get a look at him."

"She doesn't mention him," said Penny, her face taking on the anxious look which Francie had learned to associate in her friend with any thought of Uncle Jim. "It's wicked of me, I know, but I almost hope he doesn't."

On half-term holiday Fairfields had a gala look. Some of the girls had gone so far as to lay aside their uniforms, and the school grounds were gay with an unwonted number of male and female strangers strolling over the lawns and courts with their chattering daughters. Miss Maitland held court in her drawing room with parents who came to sit and drink a cup of tea with the headmistress while they discussed the weather, politics, the rationing system, anything in fact but what was really in their minds: the scholastic careers of their children. Lesser mistresses wandered about being gracious, and Matron was busy answering questions about health. It was all very typical, but new to Francie, and she watched the procedure with amusement until she was called down to the Hall by Penelope, who was all of a flutter.

"They've come, Francie, so let's go to meet them. Oh dear, Uncle Jim's there too. Isn't it a bore!"

"You needn't be afraid," said Francie staunchly. "I'll tackle him if he gets difficult."

"No, no, that's just what I don't like—any sort of a scene. Now, Francie, promise me you won't do anything or I'll pretend I have a sore throat. I swear I will," cried Penelope.

"Silly! Of course I promise," said Francie. "You must be in a dither, Penny, when you can't take a feeble joke."

"Well, I *am* in a dither," admitted Penny. "So would you be." They smoothed their hair and went down the stairs to meet the parents.

Mrs. Stewart, Penelope's mother, was quite like what Francie had expected. She was a pretty, fair-haired woman, rather retiring in her manner.

FRANCIE

Penny was like her in appearance, but even though she was so much younger the daughter seemed in a way more downright and responsible than the mother.

"Penny's quite self-sufficient," thought Francie, "whereas her mother isn't."

The famous Uncle Jim was a tall, thin man with high cheekbones, piercing dark eyes under thick brows, and bristling dark hair shot with gray. He was more attractive than Francie would have expected; Penelope's tales had given her a mental picture of a devilish monster, but Uncle Jim might have stood in for one of the modern heroes of the movies—taciturn, commanding and ruthless. It was impossible to take umbrage at his manner of greeting the girls, unless Francie chose to resent his assumption that they were *little* girls. "And I could scarcely do that," she admitted to herself, "because one can see he treats his wife exactly the same as he does us. I guess he thinks no woman has good sense."

"Come along, you women," said Uncle Jim just then, with a genial contempt, and herded them through the door and into the car. "You can chin to your hearts' content as we go."

Chin they did. Mrs. Stewart was in her gentle way a chatterbox. She had a wealth of small news items for Penny's ears, bits of gossip about their local Women's Institute, the domestic kitten, the char, and the bazaar which was soon to be held on behalf of some church mission. Now and then

Uncle Jim, though he never took his eyes off the road, contributed with gruff humor to the conversation. He was every inch the indulgent husband and parent who had taken the day off to do his duty to the family. His manner toward Francie was impeccable. And yet . . .

"He's a bully," reflected the American. "A hearthstone bully."

There were many little ways in which he showed this tendency, and she began looking out for them and balefully counting them up. When the party arrived in town and parked the car near the hotel, Uncle Jim ordered his wife and stepdaughter to bring their coats inside. He didn't suggest it, he *ordered* it. "Bring those garments and the rest of the gear with you," he said, waving toward the coats and sweaters that weren't being worn.

Francie reacted immediately. "If you lock the car door, what's the difference?" she demanded.

He flashed her a glance out of his dark eyes, as if surprised at being questioned. She gathered he wasn't used to it. "Plenty of cases of burglary, locks or no locks," he said after a slight pause. Then, just as if he had quelled a rebellion, he left the women to pick up their paraphernalia and slam the car door for themselves while he walked ahead to the inn. At the table, he picked up the menu and studied it, evidently about to order lunch for all four of them without asking their preferences.

Penny put in a hesitant suggestion. "Please,

Uncle Jim, I think Francie might like to look at the card."

"Eh? Oh—yes, of course. I forgot we aren't all in the family," he said, relinquishing the menu.

Rather stormily, Francie took pleasure in ordering a different dish from the one he had decided would be best for all of them. Then she held the card out to Penny and said, "What would *you* like, Penny?" But Penny did not take her cue. She hurriedly returned the menu to Uncle Jim and accepted his choice with outward meekness.

The day went on according to the customary schedule for half-term. They drove a short distance into the country for tea, and at the proper time Mrs. Stewart produced a packed picnic basket. Only once was the dangerous subject of the theater broached, and it was Francie who carelessly introduced it, when Mrs. Stewart asked them for some account of what was taking up their time at school.

"We've started early on *A Midsummer Night's Dream,* you know," she said eagerly, "and Penny's taken hold amazingly well. I do think it's going to be a good production in spite of how awful schoolgirls usually are about rehearsals. Penny's so good at directing, Mrs. Stewart. She coaxes them and scares them and bullies them until they're good actors in spite of themselves—but you'll see, of course, on breaking-up day. You'll be proud of her!"

Silence, heavy and uncomfortable, had fallen over the other three, but not until Francie paused for breath did she realize she had done the forbidden thing. Penny was staring unhappily at the teapot, while her mother looked frightened, avoiding the gaze of her husband. Uncle Jim was plainly angry. At least his face looked slightly flushed, which was a bad sign. Francie could have kicked herself. But now that she was into the subject she wouldn't back out.

"Utter nonsense," said Uncle Jim. "When you consider the fees you pay, Evelyn, it's shocking the girls should be encouraged to waste their time in such a manner."

"But it's such good training!" cried the irrepressible Francie. "Why, some of those little girls actually learn to enjoy Shakespeare, where they never would otherwise. There's nothing like acting to make you appreciate the lines. And Penny is so talented, it would be a shame not to develop her. Miss West says——"

"Penny could do with a little development in a few other directions." Uncle Jim's tone cut Francie short. Remembering her promise to Penny she did not retort, but inwardly she was fuming.

"He's a really cold fish," she thought. "Penny's up against something big there. What a perfectly awful man!"

Everyone was quiet on the drive back, and even Francie felt depressed.

FRANCIE

The morning started out beautifully, on the day everything happened at once. If Francie had been on the lookout for omens she might have noticed one before she was out of bed. She had waked early for some mysterious reason and saw the red shreds of sunrise streaking across a sky that was beginning to burn with a bright midsummer blue. She wasn't expecting anything fateful to happen, however, and the significance of a red sky at morning rang no bell in her mind. That mind was busy with trifles.

"We've got to have more cheesecloth," she said to Penny when they met on the way down to breakfast. "I've thought of a marvelous new arrangement for Titania's flower-bank, but I'll need about twelve yards more of cheesecloth."

"It's called butter-muslin here," said Penny in rather distant tones.

"Oh bother, I suppose it is, but I can never remember. I knew the name had something to do with dairies in both countries, and that's . . . What's the matter, Penny, are you running a temperature or something? You look so red, and your eyes——"

"It's all right. To tell you the truth, I didn't sleep very much," said Penelope. "Got a letter yesterday that upset me, that's all. Uncle Jim's put my name down for that school. I'm trying to decide whether to break off now with home or wait until the last minute for the revolt."

"Oh, Penny, how awful."

They walked along the corridor in silence. "Well, never mind," said Penny at last. "Let's think about our work. What about this butter-muslin? I suppose we could go in to Farham this afternoon and buy it in plenty of time to catch the five-thirty bus back."

"That's what I thought," said Francie. "Sure you don't mind coming? I expect I could get somebody else if you do."

The Sixth Form girls were permitted to go into town without adult company on such little expeditions, though Miss Maitland insisted that they travel in pairs. Francie and Penelope agreed in the end to meet at three o'clock at the gate.

The morning post was delivered about breakfast time, and Francie's heart gave a bound when she saw the letter that was put down at her plate. It was addressed in Glenn's writing and had been posted only four days earlier, in New York, but when she opened the envelope and read it, a sense of even greater excitement swept over her.

"Hiya, Francie!" Glenn had written. "At last, at last we're setting sail tomorrow, Bob Chapman and the Jeepers Creepers and me. Earlier than we expected. We ought to land in England on June twenty-first. As soon as we get the car ashore and I find my bearings I'll send you a telegram or card, or I'll phone, letting you know when to expect us. . . ."

"But *today's* the twenty-second," Francie said to

herself. She studied the date on the letter; it had been written ten days before. "Some dopey friend was supposed to mail it and forgot," she decided. "Well, never mind, it won't be long now!"

She tried to find Penny to share her news, but the bell for prayers had rung.

All morning Francie waited for some word, neglected her lessons, and felt more and more nervous. Of course Glenn's ship might be late, she reminded herself; she hadn't had time to look it up under the shipping news, thanks to the unknown friend's tardy mailing of the letter.

"It'll be absolutely wonderful to see him," she thought. "I'd never have thought I could get so thrilled, just at the prospect of a date. I must get Penny in on this, for Bob." Bob wasn't the favorite with her that Glenn was, but Penny might like him. It would take her mind off Uncle Jim. They could drive over to do a little sightseeing—the Cathedral maybe, if Glenn thought he'd like to do that—and eat dinner at some pub, and maybe find a movie that wasn't too old.

She found a note from Penny in the history class saying it was all right about the trip that afternoon to buy butter-muslin; Miss Maitland had been notified, and she approved. Glenn's letter had put all that matter out of Francie's head. "That's all right," she decided. "We can buy that butter-muslin anywhere, in any place we come through, if only I don't forget with all the excitement."

Word came at last, during the rest period just

after lunch; Miss Frances Nelson was wanted on the telephone, said the housemaid. It wasn't a usual thing for girls to receive telephone calls, and everyone stared at Francie as she raced out of the dormitory to the telephone, which was in a half-walled-off cloakroom in Hall.

"Francie?" came Glenn's well-remembered voice. "Is that Francie Nelson?"

"Glenn! How *are* you?" she shrieked.

"Well, thank goodness," said Glenn. "I've never had a harder time in my life with Mr. Bell's new invention, the telephone. Listen, sweetness, where is this place of yours? I'm calling from—say, Bob, what's the name of this joint? Oh yes, the King's Arms, in Kingston. Do you know the place?"

"Of course I do," said Francie. "Kingston's only fifteen miles from our market town. It shouldn't take you very long to get over here."

"Is that so? Well, listen," said Glenn.

"I'm listening."

"I don't mean listen," he said with irritation. "I just mean—will it be all right? Don't you have to get permission or something from your teacher? What I mean to say, I understand these schools are sometimes like the reform schools at home, and you can't get out without three certificates of sanity and a can opener. Yours isn't like that, by any chance?"

"Oh no," said Francie with assurance. "Nothing like that." She didn't pause to think of what she was saying, she was so eager to see Glenn. In a

188

more thoughtful mood she might have considered that she didn't really know what the rules were about dates. It was a subject which had never come up among the girls there, as far as she knew.

"Don't you even have to get permission to come out?" insisted Glenn.

"Oh, that. Yes, I guess I do."

"Well, snap into it. Our schedule's been altered, I'm sorry to say," Glenn said. "Bob's old man insists on our meeting him in France in about three days. It doesn't give us as much time as I'd planned on. So you pull up your garters and get permission without wasting time, will you?"

"Why—yes, I could do that. Right now, you mean, while you wait?"

"That would be best, wouldn't it?" said Glenn. "Run along and I'll hang on at this end. I'm sitting in a big leather chair, so I don't mind."

Francie went rushing through the passage in search of her form mistress. As though Fate were determined to save time for her, she encountered Miss Maitland just around the first corner; that was fortunate, she felt, as Miss Maitland was in any case the final court of appeal. Too much absorbed in her own affairs to pay due attention, she failed to see the wrinkle of disapproval that marred the headmistress's brow. Miss Maitland did not like her girls running in the house.

"Oh, Miss Maitland! A very dear old friend of mine has just arrived from America. I wanted permission to go out with him, and maybe to ask one

FRANCIE

of the other girls to come as well. That will be all right, won't it? I'm sorry it's so sudden, but I wasn't sure until just now when he was arriving."

"A dear old friend?" Miss Maitland stood very still, repeating the words. "A friend of your father's?" she added.

"No, that is, he knows Pop too of course, but he's my friend really. You see he's only a young boy, my age."

Miss Maitland stared, rather stupidly, thought Francie. "Just what was it, then, that you wished to do for him, Frances? Invite him here? If so, I——"

"Well, of course I'd be awfully glad to see him here too," said Francie insincerely. "I'm sure he'd be delighted to call. But right now I'd thought that as it's sort of short notice we might go out driving instead, so I could show him a little of the country. You see this is his first trip to England and he hasn't got much time."

Miss Maitland said nothing for a moment. She didn't seem to know what she wanted to say. At last, "Hadn't I better get in touch with your father about this?" she asked brightly. "Yes, I think that would be best, before we make any rash decisions. I quite realize that in America this sort of thing might be——"

"Oh, that will be all right as far as Pop's concerned, Miss Maitland. He knows all about Glenn's coming over. I wrote to him about it a long time ago."

"Perhaps, but nevertheless——"

"He *does* know," insisted Francie, who was irritated by that "perhaps." It sounded as if Miss Maitland didn't believe her. "Pop's always known Glenn. Glenn comes from my own home town, do you see; my aunt knows him and thinks he's a very nice boy, and she plays bridge with his people and everything. I tell you he wrote to me months ago about coming over this spring, and I told Pop about it then."

Miss Maitland smiled. "In that case it is quite simple, Frances. You need only get written permission from your father, and I shall make no further objection to your seeing this young man. Ordinarily I would not approve such behavior in one of my girls, but I do realize you have been accustomed to a greater amount of freedom than most of us here, and as it is such an unusual occasion——"

"I'm afraid that wouldn't do at all, Miss Maitland."

"Wouldn't *do?*" Miss Maitland's voice rose incredulously.

"No, because Pop's in Iran or maybe Iraq—I forget which it was to be this week—but there wouldn't be nearly time enough to get a letter to him and another one back."

"In that case, Frances, there is nothing to do about it. Another time, when you have received a letter of permission——"

"Another time?" Francie's voice, too, was rising. "But there won't *be* another time. Glenn's only got three days in England. There isn't even time to send Pop a cable."

Miss Maitland did not reply. Her expression was unyielding.

"I don't see why you can't believe me," continued Francie. "I've assured you——"

"Those are the rules, Frances. I'm very sorry, but there it is."

"But——" Francie struggled with a mixture of incredulity and rage. It was, really, too humiliating and exasperating! She tried again, this time in dignified tones. "Miss Maitland, I'm not accustomed to telling lies to people. When I've assured you, over and over again, that my father does really know and like this boy——"

"And I, Frances, am not accustomed to being questioned on my rules of discipline." The headmistress's voice cut like a knife. "*I* am head of Fairfields School, a fact you have evidently forgotten. We will now drop this discussion, if you please." She swept off down the passage.

Francie stood there as if frozen. She was not frozen, however.

On the contrary, she burned with pure temper; she was feverish. Never, never in her whole life had anyone spoken to her like that. Never before had her word been doubted (she was convinced that the headmistress had doubted her word). Never had she been so abruptly thwarted.

At first she forgot the cause of the dispute, and was aware only that she hated Miss Maitland and detested the school, and that she must without more delay get out of Fairfields. She clenched her fists, obsessed with a vision of immediate flight. Second thoughts made her pause. She was friendless in England just at the moment—Pop was out of touch, and Aunt Lolly was away. There was only Glenn.

Good heavens, Glenn! He must still be there, patiently hanging on to the telephone. At least she earnestly hoped he was; she must explain and make some excuse. What was she to say? It was necessary to think of something on the instant. She would tell a lie, she would do anything rather than risk another, worse humiliation such as having him arrive all trustful at Fairfields only to be turned away by Miss Maitland. *Oh!* It was too awful!

The thought of explaining the true state of affairs crossed her mind, but she dismissed it immediately. She simply could not go back to the telephone like a little whipped puppy and confess that she wasn't allowed to see him—she, Francie Nelson, forbidden to see her own boy friend! All the way from America, too!

Dimly she felt another emotion, a perfectly natural grief and frustration at the thought of missing Glenn's visit. She had depended on it more than she realized. As soon as she knew he was coming she had felt more cheerful about all the pinpricks of existence at Fairfields. Nothing sweetens a long trial so much as the knowledge that there is a limit, a known date one can make a ring around on the calendar to mark a break in the tiresome routine.

Moreover, it was all so unjust. No one knew better than Francie how really all right it would have been for her to go out with Glenn. When had anyone before told her that she should not? Pop was far less easy in these matters than Aunt Norah had been, but even Pop liked Glenn and took their companionship for granted. It would have been so easy, too, to get his written permission! How was she to know that such a silly, unnecessary complication would arise? Pop would feel so sorry for her; Francie nearly burst into tears as she thought of Pop's pity.

In the meantime, here were the minutes ticking off and Glenn still waiting. What to do?

Down the corridor at this moment came Penelope of all people, so sunk in troubled thought that she saw nothing unusual about Francie's flushed cheeks and stormy eyes. She only said absently, "There you are; I wondered what had become of you. Don't forget we're catching that three o'clock bus."

"So we are!"

Penny went on down the corridor and Francie remained where she was, looking as if she had made a discovery, as indeed she had. Salvation had suddenly opened before her. The bus and the town!

She ran back to the telephone at last. "Hello," she said breathlessly. "Are you still there?"

"I am, sugar, but only just," said Glenn. "Where did you go? Did you take a bath, or what? I must owe about ten dollars or pounds sterling or something on this call."

"I'm sorry, but it's hard to fix things up over in this country. Nobody hurries."

"I'm finding that out," said Glenn.

"Well, listen," said Francie. "I've got it all figured out now. It just happens Penny and I have got to go in to Farham this afternoon, so we might as well meet you there instead of here. Farham—F-a-r-h-a-m. Got it? It's only a short run from Kingston and anybody will tell you. Penny and I are taking the bus and we can meet you at the local pub, the Crown. Outside, not inside; we wouldn't be allowed to go in in our school uniforms."

"That's funny," said Glenn.

"Yes, maybe, but let's not talk about it now." Francie's ears had detected a footstep near the telephone booth. "We'll meet you there about three-thirty," she said hastily. " 'Bye now."

CHAPTER 10

"I'M AFRAID I don't really understand even yet," said Penny at last. "You'll have to begin over again, this time at the beginning. Do try not to get so excited, Francie. Half the time I can't make any sense out of it at all."

The two girls stood near the gate of Fairfields in the bright afternoon sunlight, waiting for the bus. They had been there for several minutes and all that time Francie had been talking with feverish indignation. At these words she groaned.

"I wish you'd listen carefully," she said. "We won't be able to talk in the bus if there's anybody else there. Even now——" She paused and looked over the fence cautiously. "Somebody might be around in the bushes, listening," she explained. "It's terribly hard to tell anything in confidence around here."

"But where *are* these boys? Why all this secrecy?"

"They're driving over in their car to Farham and meeting us there."

"Why are they doing that?" asked Penny calmly.

"I've just told you, Miss Maitland said I couldn't go out with them unless I had Pop's written permission, and I haven't got it and she knows I haven't, and I can't get it either, not until Glenn's gone. Written permission, did you ever hear anything so ridiculous? After I told her and told her that it *would* be all right with Pop! Wouldn't you think she might take my word?"

Penelope thought about it. "She might, but she's not used to parents like your Pop," she decided at last. "She's more used to parents like my Uncle Jim. Besides, Francie, those are the rules. You wouldn't find many headmistresses who'd be any more indulgent than Miss Maitland."

"But it means I'd have *missed seeing Glenn!*"

"Yes, but just the same——"

Francie turned away angrily. "I thought *you'd* understand. You, anyway. Out of all these people . . ."

Penny struggled with herself for a moment and then said, "Yes, I do understand, Francie. I can see why you're so furious. I'll even admit that if I were American I'd be furious too."

"Then you don't mind that we're going to meet them?" demanded Francie. "You're not angry?"

"Oh no. Not angry. Just—well, I realize you might not understand what it's like, defying a headmistress."

"You're right I don't. *I'm* not afraid," said Francie loftily, and Penny in spite of herself laughed. "But I'm worried for you," added Francie. "I don't want to get you into trouble."

"You needn't be; I can take care of myself," said Penny.

"Then you don't feel I've dragged you into something?"

Francie's anxious tones touched her friend deeply. Penny replied on impulse, "I'll see you through, Francie. I'm with you, no matter what happens."

The American girl's grateful smile was enough to make Penny forget her misgivings. But she looked thoughtful as the bus came in view and they climbed into it.

There were a few other passengers, and the girls did not dare to talk about the affair on the way in to Farham. Francie, staring with unseeing eyes at the summer fields they went bowling past, tried to imagine what Glenn would think of all this uproar if he knew. Should she tell him in a joking way, or would it be better not to confess anything? That would depend, no doubt, on how much confession would be necessary; unknowing, he might expect to be asked into the school when the meeting was accomplished. She decided to wait and see what happened.

It was an uneasy business altogether. If Penny had not suggested that they fill in the waiting-time buying their butter-muslin, Francie would have bitten her nails to the quick. As it was, they did not linger too long near the pub, an exercise which Penny felt would make them dangerously conspicuous, dressed as they were in their uniforms and straw hats with school ribbons around them. The girls had just crossed the street, Francie carrying the butter-muslin in a bulky brown-paper parcel, when a gleaming American car, an open model, drove up to the curb.

"Whoopee! There they are!" cried Francie, forgetting all caution and breaking into a run. Glenn stepped from the car, and when after the second look he recognized her he rushed forward and hugged her in full view of the High Street.

"How are you anyway? Gee, it's good to see you!" he cried. "I wasn't sure it was you for a minute in that outfit."

Bob Chapman, a tall young man with an attractively solemn look and rather curly dark hair, was out of the car on Glenn's heels. He and Francie exchanged quick greetings and then Penelope had to be introduced to the boys, while excitement ran high all around. Glenn interrupted his own chatter at last.

"Why are we all standing here?" he demanded. "Can't we go somewhere and sit? Isn't there anywhere at all you girls are allowed to rest?"

"Oh, we could have tea in the hotel, I suppose. It's just the pub I've got to keep out of," explained Francie. "Or we could go to the tearoom down the street. It's a potty little place, but——"

"Honestly, Francie, I don't know about that." Penelope was trying to signal her friend tactfully as she spoke. "Everybody around here knows we're from Fairfields. Just in case there's any trouble do you feel we ought to give them something more to talk about? They'll have plenty as it is."

Francie stopped to think. Bob said, "Well, then, let's all pile into the bus and go somewhere else, why don't we?"

"Oh, we couldn't do that," said Penny.

"Why in the world not?" said Glenn in surprise. "What else can we do?"

Helplessly Penny looked toward Francie to explain. What Glenn had suggested was so outrageous that she felt Francie must be able to see for herself that it was impossible. Francie must act as interpreter between England and America; Penny herself could not begin to do it. To her horror Francie only said easily, "Oh, it's against the rules to go riding without special permission, but as practically everything's against the rules anyway at that school, I guess a little more rule-breaking won't matter."

"Penny doesn't seem so sure," Bob pointed out.

"Oh, Penny's a good sport. She says she'll stand by, no matter what," said Francie blithely.

Penny stood there on the pavement, watching Francie climb into the car. She had never in her life been in such a predicament. A whirl of doubts and fears kept her dumb; the only thing that stood out in the confusion was what Francie had just said: "She says she'll stand by, no matter what." Well, and so Penny *had* said it. There was nothing she could do now, except regret Francie's ignorance of the common laws of self-preservation. Penny climbed into the car.

"We'd better take off our hats as soon as we're out of town," said Francie. "No need to advertise where we're from."

Still miserably silent, Penny agreed.

They decided there was time to go as far as the sea for their tea, and they could be back in ample time to catch the bus. Penny revived a little, and took part in the discussion. The girls talked it over for a long time while the boys waited impatiently, and the car idled on the road outside Farham.

"Personally I don't care what we do while we talk," Glenn said about three times, "as long as we *can* talk. Do you realize I haven't seen this girl in six months, about?"

"Well, Penny thinks we ought to take you to the Museum, but I say you'd be bored," said Francie. "It's not so easy to think of things to do, Glenn. There aren't any juke-box joints here, you know, and it's hard to catch a good picture. As for television——"

"Who cares about all that? You'll have Penny here calling us all barbarians," said Bob. "Did we or didn't we come over to Europe to see the old country as she really is? Well then, juke me no juke boxes. Let's keep going until we get somewhere, that's all, and don't forget the traffic regulations."

"It does feel odd, not worrying about petrol," sighed Penny gratefully. The girls had taken off their hats and hidden them; now the breeze blew through their hair and filled them with adventurous delight.

In the back seat Penny even relaxed a little and began to enjoy Bob's company. Glenn drove, with Francie in the seat beside him and all the way they chattered. Ruth was doing fine, Glenn reported, and Gretta was all wet, though a good enough kid once you got to know her. One boy they knew well had failed his math exam and would have to pass an entrance exam before he was allowed into State. The newest excitement was wagering about who would "make" this fraternity or that. Aunt Norah was expected back from Florida in plenty of time to get the house ready for Francie's return. None of the crowd went to the Chocolate Shoppe any more. There'd been a switch of management and they preferred a chop-suey place farther downtown.

"Oh, golly, but it will be fun to get back," sighed Francie.

"It'll be fun having you back," said Glenn emphatically. "It's not the same without you. Say, though, you look fine, except for that gosh-awful outfit. Younger somehow."

"Is that good? I must be perfectly terrible to look at. Nothing done to my hair in weeks, and no makeup."

"You look okay," he said heartily. "Say, do you

know you're beginning to talk sort of Englishy? You are, honestly. 'Frightful dress,'" he said, mimicking her tone. "You'll probably start a new style of speech in Jefferson."

Francie shrieked with laughter, conscious that Penny was watching her with indulgent amusement when she wasn't chattering with Bob in the back seat of the car. It was easy to forget for the moment that they weren't in America where there were no Miss Maitlands to return to, and no Cinderella-like rush to be home on time.

When they reached the beach it was necessary to drive a little farther than they had expected, in order to find a café open. It was still rather early in the season and most of the places were closed and boarded up, but at last they found a teashop that would serve them, and there they sat for a long time, eating stale cakes and ice cream, and drinking tea.

"This is terrible stuff," said Glenn, looking at his plate with disfavor. "Do they feed you like this everywhere in England?"

"Now don't start talking about double malteds," said Penny warningly. "It's an old joke here, the way you Americans begin to long for your soda fountains. Francie's a little better than she was, but for a while she was a great trial to all of us."

"That's what I say," added Bob. He spoke with deadly seriousness. "You ought to take things the way you find them in foreign countries, Glenn.

What will these people think of us if we go criticizing everything about them just because it's not like home?"

"Hear, hear," said Francie, applauding. "Shame on you, Glenn!"

Bob looked puzzled by their laughter until Penny explained: "We're only pulling your leg. I lived in America myself, so I don't really mind a little harmless yearning for a chocolate soda."

"To tell the truth, it's all a lot better than we'd been led to expect. I thought I'd be really hungry by this time," said Glenn.

"Oh no, it's not so bad. There's food enough to eat. Only it's stodgy, most of the time, and pretty much the same every day," said Francie, "and naturally people who keep house get tired of planning and contriving. You see it's like being poor all the time, with no hope of it getting any better, at least not for a long while. When you're poor in America you've always got the saving hope that tomorrow you just might, miraculously, strike it rich. Nobody in England feels like that."

"There aren't any miracles in England, eh?" asked Bob. "I see. I don't know as I'd like that. How do most of you feel about it?"

Penny, to whom he addressed his question, said, "We've never believed as much in miracles as Americans do. I suppose we feel we've got to pull through, that's all. We've always done it and we feel we ought to keep on trying."

"Kind of a grim outlook," said Glenn soberly.

"Take it all in all, I guess Europe's no picnic. That's about the size of it."

All four young people were grave and silent for a little. Penny suddenly noted the café clock and exclaimed in dismay. "Francie! Do look at the time. We'll never be back in Farham in time for that bus!"

Francie's hand fluttered to her mouth in alarm. Already it was nearly five o'clock. They all looked at each other, wondering what they should do about the predicament.

"I could get you back to the school, but it's bound to be a little late," suggested Glenn. "Would anyone notice?"

"We'd be half an hour late. They'd be sure to notice," said Francie. "Wait a minute, let me think." She covered her eyes with her hands and sat as if in a trance, while the others respectfully waited. "I know," she said at last, taking her hands down. "I'll manage. Just leave it to me."

Penny looked dubious, but said nothing while Francie asked the waitress where she could find a telephone. There was a public one, said the waitress, in a little booth just down the beach and across the road. Francie collected loose change from the boys and hurried out the door purposefully.

"What's she going to do?" asked Glenn.

"I don't know," said Penny in worried tones. "I hope she's not getting in too deep."

"But you'll get into trouble too, won't you?" Bob asked.

FRANCIE

"Oh well . . ." Her voice trailed off. The boys looked at her in respectful silence, but they had no idea of how deeply terrified she was. Penny had too much self-control for that.

Francie returned after a little while and nodded in a reassuring manner at her friend. "It's all right for the moment," she said, picking up another cake. "Nothing to worry about."

"How did you fix it? What did you say?" asked Penny tensely.

"Oh, I talked to Ella." Ella was the maid. "I didn't have to say much, fortunately, because the girl at the switchboard didn't tell them at the other end where I was calling from. You know they sometimes do; she just asked if that was the Fairfields number, and said, 'Wait a minute,' and said to me, 'Fourpence please,' and I think Ella's too dumb to notice that fourpence is too much for a strictly local call."

"Yes," said Penny, "but just what did you say? You didn't lie, did you?"

"Of course I didn't lie," said Francie, with indignation in her tones. "I only didn't tell the whole truth. I said we were awfully sorry but we'd missed the bus, and would she tell somebody, please, and we'd get some supper and be along later."

Penny didn't speak until Bob said, "Do you think you can get by with that?"

"No," Penny said, "I don't think so. There's going to be a row."

"I must say, you're awfully calm about it." He looked curiously at her pale face.

"Sufficient unto the day," said Francie, waving a macaroon in the air. "The thing is, I'm so awfully fed up I don't much care, and Penny feels the same way for reasons of her own. Do you know, they tried to stop me seeing you boys at all?"

"No fooling!" Glenn had to hear the whole story then, and Francie retailed it with enthusiasm.

"So you see, I've burned my boats, or if I haven't it doesn't really make the slightest difference," she finished recklessly. "I couldn't care less."

"What about Penny, though?" demanded Bob. "She's got more to lose, it seems to me. We're not *her* old friends from America."

They looked expectantly at the English girl, who only shook her head.

"Penny's backing me up," insisted Francie. "Still, maybe we'd better be more careful from now on, and get home pretty early."

A spin in the country, perhaps a stop somewhere for a sandwich, and back to school before nine o'clock would give them plenty of time to prepare for what would certainly be an ordeal of explanations, they decided. "Though if we just say we took a car back," said Francie, "they may not probe further. I should think it most unlikely they'd make too much fuss; we're big girls now, even in their estimation. Oh, never mind. Let's forget about it now and just have fun."

Penny swallowed hard and attempted to take this advice.

It had been a most exciting and enjoyable evening, in spite of the worry which even the impenitent Francie could not quite banish from her mind. They had driven far and fast, had eaten a surprisingly good dinner at a wayside hotel, and had been busy since, the girls telling the boys a wealth of things about England. They had chattered until their throats were dry. Now with an early moon making the fields silver, they drove slowly along the deserted road, talking in low tones.

"It's been a wonderful start to my trip, seeing you like this, Francie," said Glenn with a sigh. "Gosh, I wish you could come on with us to France. I can't tell you what a difference it makes to Jefferson, not having you there."

This was most gratifying. Francie said, "Don't think it hasn't made a difference to me too. I could have howled sometimes, I was so homesick for the gang."

"Honest? I didn't know how you might be feeling after all this time. Those boys you talked about in your letter to Ruth—Mark and Peter—didn't they make you forget all about us?"

"Oh no, Glenn, never for a minute. They're cute enough, but I'm not used to English boys, I guess. And anyway I haven't had much chance to get acquainted. It's different over here."

"Well, I'm mighty glad to find you haven't changed that way."

"What do you mean, that way?" she asked with a flicker of interest. "Have I changed any way at all?"

"Gosh, yes," said Glenn readily. "You're a lot different. You look younger, and you're keener on things, and not so, well, so spoiled. I guess what I mean is that you're a lot nicer to me!"

"That's because I'm so glad to see somebody from home!"

"Poor kid," said Glenn.

It took a little while for these words and their true significance to soak into Francie's brain. When they did she suddenly sat up to attention. "Did you say poor kid? Why?" she demanded.

"Why?" repeated Glenn. "Oh, I don't know. I guess I've been feeling awfully sorry for you. It's only natural. We're all sorry for you, back at Jefferson."

"But why should you be *sorry* for me? This I don't like."

"Well, gee, haven't you been awfully unhappy? You sounded it. You kept writing letters . . ." His voice trailed off.

"I have *not* been unhappy," said Francie in clear tones. "I love England, as a matter of fact."

Glenn turned to look at her incredulously. "Go on! You couldn't. Stuck away in that crummy school——"

"And what's the matter with Fairfields? It's a very good school and I'm happy there. Sure, they don't always look at things my way and I don't see things in theirs, but it's a very nice gang of girls, Glenn, and don't you forget it. Why, they're worth any number of the kids at home, in lots of ways. I can't tell you all about it straight off . . ." Nor could she, she reflected. It would take hours and perhaps more words than she knew to explain Jennifer's sturdy independence, the honest friendship of Wendy or Marcie, the sincerity of all of them. They had good sense, those girls, and they were kind. At least, all except Jennifer were kind, and she had other qualities. "They're tough," said Francie aloud. "Lots tougher than we are. And better sports, as far as I can see. I know that's a soppy expression but it's what I mean. I mean, it's not easy to tell in America what people are like, is it? Things are so easy there. Here, you can see right away . . . But I didn't mean to make a speech, Glenn. I only wanted you to understand, I *like* England."

"You don't have to apologize. I'm having a swell time," said Glenn. "Say—" he lowered his voice, his head leaning toward her as he drove very slowly— "is Penny enjoying herself, do you think?"

"Oh yes. She's having a wonderful time. Why?"

"I just wondered. She's a nice kid, isn't she? Anyway Bob thinks so. I guess he's fallen for her. Is there anybody here she's keen on? He asked me to find out, back there where we had dinner."

"I shouldn't think so. Penny's set on her work more than anything, and right now her head's full of plans for the future. Her stepfather is absolutely the *worst*—listen and I'll tell you."

In conspiratorial whispers she confided to Glenn the particulars of Penny's family troubles.

The car idled along a seaside road. Now and then someone sounded a warning horn and went sweeping past them in the dark, but traffic was not heavy. In the back seat, the other young people were talking animatedly of certain famous stage productions they had witnessed in New York.

"To think Penny and I should be having a double date here in the heart of England!" murmured Francie dreamily. "Who would have expected this when I woke up this morning?"

"I hate to be a spoilsport," said Penny at last, "but we've got to go back now, Francie, if we ever expect to get in at all. They lock the doors when it's time to turn out the lights." She spoke with determined cheerfulness, though inside she was quaking.

"Yes, I know." Francie moved reluctantly from her comfortable position against Glenn's shoulder. They had been watching the moonlight on the sea for some time.

"It's true, Glenn, we'll have to get going."

"Oh, gee," said Glenn. "Well, it's been nice while it lasted, and I'm sure glad you were both willing to take the chance."

They drove rapidly now along the road toward Fairfields, the setting moon making their shadows grotesquely long on the white road. Francie struck a match to look at her watch. They would make it, she decided, just in good time. They would put on their hats, carry the butter-muslin parcel, and simply stroll through the front door, trusting to luck and good nature to carry them past the first awkward moments. It might be best to get out of the car a fairly good distance from the gates, of course, and not to talk loud to the boys, just in case someone was out in the grounds, snooping. . . .

The car sneezed, faltered, recovered, and then with a more noticeable sneeze came to a halt.

"What have you done to her?" demanded Bob, peering over the back of the seat.

"Nothing I shouldn't have," said Glenn indignantly. "What do you think? Here, let me turn on the light . . . Empty! Didn't you fill her up at Kingston the way I told you?"

"Nope. Don't you remember, the filling station was closed?"

Glenn groaned. "Of all the boneheaded stunts," he said. "To run out of gas on our first day!"

"Oh, my goodness," said Francie. "What do we do now?" Penny only gasped. She had known it all along, she told herself. Something like this was bound to happen, by all the laws of retribution.

"Find a filling station, I guess," Glenn said. "One

FRANCIE

of us will have to walk along and trust to luck it won't be too far away. How far back did we pass one, does anybody remember?"

"I haven't seen a station since we left the place where we ate," said Penny flatly. "It's not so easy to find them here in the country, you know. Oh dear, what a mess!"

"One of the boys will have to thumb a ride, that's all," said Francie.

"Yes, but what with? There hasn't been a car along here for the past half hour," Bob reminded her. "I think I'll get out and start walking ahead, and take my chances."

Bob got started and the others settled back to wait. There was nothing else to do, they agreed. Penny was too well disciplined to speak of the first thought in her mind: the galloping minutes, and the nemesis that waited for them at Fairfields if they should be late. Even the light-hearted Francie was depressed. It was hard to talk cheerfully as they waited for Bob to come back.

Time went on and on. At first there was a little hope, then after a while there wasn't any. The doors at Fairfields would be locked. Francie squinted at her watch; she thought she could see Penny trying to look at hers, though neither of them said anything.

"Where can Bob have gone to?" asked Glenn in peevish tones. "He's been away an hour. What does he think he's doing?"

Penny said, "He won't find it too easy, you know. Nowadays there isn't much pleasure motoring, because there's such a small ration, and people buy their petrol in tiny amounts—three gallons at a time or even less."

Glenn whistled. "Then naturally they don't keep a lot on hand. Is that it?"

"That's it. Some of the stations are simply closed down for good. And the others even if they're open in the daytime might be locked up after tea. Just now we're not a very go-ahead nation, Glenn."

"Well, but . . . Then what do you think he's going to do?"

"If he gets a lift anywhere," Francie contributed, "he'll have to telephone some big garage where they'd be keeping a man on the premises all night, and I expect that's what he's doing, waiting for a relief car. They allow hire-cars and that sort of thing, fortunately. He'll be getting a car like that to bring him back.

"That's dandy. But what is going to happen to you kids?"

"Time," said Francie, "will tell."

It seemed very late when they heard the car coming, and saw a glow around the curve of the road. It was a shock to Francie when she looked at her watch to see that it was only nine-thirty. Nine-thirty! Sometimes in Jefferson they would only just be starting out to a dance at the Country Club by that time. Yet for Fairfields it was really terribly late.

The thought of Fairfields sent a premonitory chill down her back. She exchanged a long, sober look with Penny, and then the hire-car arrived, and there was Bob bustling out of it with a petrol can.

After that they hurried in a silence that might almost be called grim. Glenn handed over coupons and money, and told Bob to get into the car, while the hire-car driver poured the gasoline into their tank. "Pretty soft for us, I guess he's thinking," said Glenn as the driver went off. "We get practically all the gasoline we want, and yet you who live here——"

"Well, that's the way they want it, or they wouldn't do it," said Francie. "Come on, Glenn, less philosophy and more action. Let's get going. Penny and I have got a lot more to go through tonight, don't forget."

"It's a shame," said Bob. "Would it help any if we came in with you and tried to explain to this she-dragon?"

"It would not," said Penny flatly. "The best thing you can do is get away before the fireworks start."

"But it seems so cowardly!"

"You can stand by if you like," said Francie. "Give us the name of your hotel, and if we're still alive tomorrow morning, and if there's time before you start off on your travels, we'll let you know how things turn out. Otherwise we'll write you in Paris. Won't we, Penny?"

"We're almost there," said Penny, who had been sitting up straight, watching the road. "Slow up,

Glenn; we don't want to drive too close . . . That's it, better stop here. Well, good night, boys. It's been charming."

Francie hastily kissed Glenn, and recovered the butter-muslin, which she had nearly forgotten. They whispered now. "Wait until we've had the chance to get indoors," she said, "and then drive off as quietly as you can, while their attention's being distracted. You never know; we may smuggle ourselves in without any noise."

On tiptoe the girls approached the house. Somewhat to their surprise, it was not blazing with lights and loud with search parties. In fact, the place looked remarkably dark. The gates stood open, but then they usually did; nobody ever closed them. Fairfields seemed fast asleep in the gathering dark as the moon was whirled around to the other side of the planet. It was almost disappointing, when they were so keyed up. Only as they drew nearer, around the corner of one of the turrets, Francie saw a light.

"That's in staff headquarters," Penny whispered when her attention was drawn to it. "It doesn't mean anything. Listen, Francie, I'm going to try the cloakroom window. It isn't often locked."

"Good egg!" Francie would never have thought of that for herself.

The cloakroom window could be reached from outside if you stepped on a sloping part of the wall underneath it. Sometimes in wet weather this could not be done because the slope was precipitous, and when it was slippery as well the thing was hopeless. Besides, you had to hang on to the ivy, and you had to pick your bit of ivy carefully. Francie was not at all sure they would be able to negotiate it, but it was worth trying. She felt a nervous desire to giggle, but stifled the impulse and with Penny crept carefully around the house to the right spot.

Penny went first. With Francie holding her around the waist she stood on the sloping bit of wall and with excruciatingly silent care she attempted to raise the sash. After a breathless moment, it went up quietly. Francie breathed easier; half the battle was won.

Carefully Penny made her way through the window, with Francie pushing her in the small of the back. Inside, she turned to help her friend; Francie could see her face, white and earnest in what was left of the moonlight. Penny held out her hand to help.

Francie took it, placed her foot on the slope, and with her other hand took firm hold of a bit of ivy. She swung up. She was going to make it—then the ivy gave way.

For a second Francie stood on one foot, wildly reaching with the other for foothold, and trying to grab Penny's wrist with her free hand. It was no use. She hung, as it were, in space, and then she fell. The crash sounded appallingly loud.

She had barely time to climb to her feet and feel herself for broken bones when a light went on in the passage beyond Penny's head. Francie, holding her breath, heard a shocked whisper inside the window, and then Miss West's voice no longer bothering to whisper.

"Penelope! What in the world are you doing here? And who is that outside?"

Francie on tiptoe pulled herself up to the window sill.

"It's me, Miss West," she said. "Please can you help me in, or open the door or something?"

CHAPTER 11

FRANCIE WOKE in the morning, blinking in sleepy, stupid surprise at her new surroundings. The sun was coming in at an unaccustomed angle and the first thing her eyes fell on was a white washstand that she could not remember having seen before.

"What in the world . . ."

Then it all poured into her consciousness at once, appallingly. She was in isolation. She and Penny were in disgrace, and had been sent to the sickroom and an unused guest room, separately, for the night. They were moral lepers. They were to stay there, Miss West had said, until she could tell Miss Maitland about their sin, and a decision could be made as to their fate.

"As if we were about eight years old," said Francie to herself scoffingly, but she could not rally her spirits with mockery. No matter how often she told herself that it couldn't make any real difference to her, she was apprehensive. Of what? She could not have said. Pop, she was sure, would not be terribly angry, because in his philosophy her crime would not seem great. He would see her point of view, she was sure. He was her Pop, her own property. That was why it had been maddeningly narrow of Miss Maitland not to take her word for it, and assume that Pop's permission would have been forthcoming if he had been asked; and Miss Maitland had been in the wrong, too, in hinting that Francie might lie to get her own way. Oh, very much in the wrong! Francie could still make herself angry at the thought of it.

And yet, and yet—hadn't Pop told her that she must try to accept the code of the place where she was living? He would take a poor view of her failure to do that. No, Pop would not be pleased, nor would he be quite whole-heartedly on her side . . . "But he won't punish me," she reassured herself. "He'll scold me, I suppose, and make me feel ashamed, but that's as far as it can go. When it comes to the point he'll back me up. And what can Miss Maitland do that would be worse? Nothing. She can kick me out, but who cares?"

The answer came, out of the middle of the sore place on Francie's conscience. Penny would care.

Francie's heart sank like a stone. Not only herself, but Penny would get into a mess. Penny would be sent home, not to an indulgent, understanding Pop, but to that mean-eyed, conceited, bigoted Uncle Jim. And just at the most critical time, too, for Penny's hopes and chances. Underneath their deliberately pessimistic forecasts, both girls had clung to the last hope of a scholarship for Penny in the dramatic school. If that came through, they had been confident, Uncle Jim would not be able to hold out. Mrs. Stewart would take her stand on Penny's side, and with the financial question settled Uncle Jim's misgivings as to the suitability of such a career would not be enough to support his objections. Now, Penny would undoubtedly be expelled. There would be no possible chance under those circumstances of a scholarship.

"And it's all my fault," mused Francie miserably. "She only came along because of me. She didn't even know what she was going to be in for, at the beginning, and then, just to show she was my friend . . ."

She jumped out of bed and began to dress, burning with anxiety to undo the harm she had done. Now at last she was really frightened.

Her toilet was completed before she remembered that Miss West had told her with severe emphasis that she must remain in that room until summoned. How could she bear the delay? She fretted like the prisoner she was. She walked up and down the room, now and then pausing to peer miserably from the window for signs of life. She had evidently waked up earlier than usual, and the time crawled along. "I *would* wake early," she thought. Moreover, the window of this room didn't overlook the driveway, so there was no method of knowing whether or not the girls were up and about, taking their exercise. The suspense grew worse and worse. What were those schoolmistresses doing all this time? Perhaps they were already at work, ruining Penny's career and her very life before Francie could so much as put in a word for the hapless victim. Oh, she could not bear it; soon she would go out of the room, orders or no orders, to find Miss Maitland and speak her mind. At the thought of Miss Maitland's face should she actually do just that, Francie giggled hysterically. The giggle was throttled in her throat; the door opened.

It was only Ella with a tray. "Good morning," said the maid, just as if everything were normal. "I've brought your breakfast. Miss West says she'll be up directly after prayers."

"Oh Ella, is Penelope all right?"

"She was quite all right just now when I took her tray in."

Francie felt Ella's subtly amused and admiring gaze, but she was in no mood for flattery. "What did Miss West say about coming up for her? Same message as mine?" she demanded.

"Yes, just the same." Ella looked over her shoulder, as if she had heard someone calling her, and hurried out.

Another hour passed, and then at last Miss West arrived. She too said "Good morning, Frances," quite calmly. Penny was with her; the mistress had evidently been sent only to collect the miscreants and not, as Francie realized in momentary relief, to discipline them. Penny looked pinched and miserable. The girls' eyes met, but they didn't speak. In a grim silence the three went down the stairs, past the murmuring classrooms, and on through the corridor to Miss Maitland's office. Francie recalled the day after the *Richard the Third* treat. Miss Maitland's scolding then was *nothing* compared to what this would be!

The headmistress sat behind a flat-topped desk, regarding them with expressionless eyes. Her hair was parted exactly in the middle, she sat at the exact middle of the desk, and her hands rested, loosely clasped, on a clean blotter. Francie's eyes went at once to the corner of the desk where stood a slender vase with a rose in it. The vase, she wanted to say, upset the balance of the symmetrical design; there should have been another one exactly like it standing at the opposite corner. Her eyes traveled erratically—she was merely trying to avoid meeting Miss Maitland's gaze—from chair to lamp to carpet, and she was absorbedly tracing out the seam of that when Miss Maitland said,

"Thank you, Miss West; you may go to your class now."

Penny and Francie stood side by side, their hands held stiffly down by their gray flannel skirts, and faced the headmistress. Francie stole a glance at Penny's white face, and began tumultuously,

"Miss Maitland, I want to——"

"Just a minute, Frances, please." Miss Maitland's words dropped like bits of clear ice. "You will have your chance to speak in good time. Now then. According to Miss West, neither of you was at school during tea yesterday, nor did you put in an appearance all evening. You had received permission, I remember, to go to Farham in the afternoon. I am given to understand that Frances telephoned at teatime to say you had both missed the bus and would return later. Is this, in the main, a correct version of what happened?"

"Yes, Miss Maitland," said Penny.

"Yes, Miss Maitland," said Francie, "but——"

"Following this," continued Miss Maitland inexorably, "the mistresses and the girls, naturally preoccupied with other affairs, did not keep a watch for you, though Miss West began to feel uneasy as bedtime approached. She sat up waiting for some time after the school had retired, and at last heard the noise of a motorcar which paused briefly not far from the gates. She presumed it was your taxi. On her way down to make certain that the front door was not locked, she was astonished"—her eyes shot a blue gleam—"astonished to encounter you, Penelope, creeping through the window, no doubt in a childish attempt to conceal your late return, with you, Frances, waiting outside on the ground. Is this what happened?"

"Yes, Miss Maitland, but I want to tell you——"

"Must I repeat, Frances, that I wish you to wait your turn?"

"No, Miss Maitland. Sorry."

"Thank you. Then I will ask Penelope first to give me an account and an explanation of your behavior throughout this escapade," said the headmistress in her chilly, impartial tones.

"Yes, Miss Maitland," said Penny. Her voice had a barely perceptible quaver, but she spoke without hesitation. "We went into Farham by the three o'clock bus and bought our butter-muslin. Then in the street we met two friends in a motorcar. We talked a little and decided to take a short ride with them."

"One moment, Penelope. Just who were these friends? People from your village?"

"No," said Penny, hesitating just a little. "They come from America."

"Ah. Old friends?"

"Not very," said Penny, twisting her fingers.

Francie nearly shouted. "They aren't Penny's friends; she never met them before; it wasn't her fault, Miss Maitland, it was——"

"You did not, in fact, know them before yesterday, Penelope?" continued Miss Maitland, without acknowledging by more than a flicker, as well as her question, that she had taken in what Francie said.

"No, Miss Maitland."

"Yet the meeting was not by chance," stated the headmistress, without making a question of it. "It was prearranged."

"Yes, Miss Maitland."

"*She* didn't know," cried Francie.

This time, however, Miss Maitland refused to register at all. She only said, "Continue, Penelope.

What happened next? I can scarcely believe that you merely toured about the country lanes for seven hours."

Haltingly Penny went on. She told how they had gone to the seaside and overstayed, how they realized too late they had missed the bus back to school, and how they went driving and stopped for more substantial food later on. Francie noticed that she made no mention of the telephone call. That, she knew, was because it was exclusively Francie's wrongdoing; Penny was trying to avoid calling Miss Maitland's attention to the telephone call. All the way through the tale, Penny had been shouldering half the blame. Was there ever such a girl? Francie felt she had never before encountered such decency, the more so since now at last it was dawning on her that the affair was truly grave. The awed expression on Penny's face and the controlled shock of Miss Maitland's countenance were something beyond her experience of scrapes at school. Francie had done more than merely break a few irksome rules. She had outraged the entire system of English education. It gave her a chill down her spine to think of it, and yet the sun poured in through the window and out of doors a hundred birds were singing in the summer warmth.

Fairfields had never seemed lovelier. Some of the girls were practicing tennis, working for the coming tournament; the sound of thumping balls and laughing remarks came to her ears. Everything and everyone outside was in the right place, doing the right thing, but here in this cold room Francie was in the wrong. She was not nearly so nice a girl as—well, as Jennifer, for example. She felt that she would never be in the right again. And Penny! She had dragged Penny with her into the outer darkness. It didn't bear thinking about, but she must think about it nevertheless.

"They'll send me away, and Penny too. I don't *want* to go away," she thought. In her distress she did not pause to wonder at this contradiction of much she had been saying for weeks. Now her sense of loss was overwhelming. It had outgrown such small misgivings as what her father might say or think.

". . . . and so," Penny was concluding her crisp, emotionless account, "we were so very late by the time we got the petrol that we thought the door would be locked. Of course we didn't want to knock up anybody, so we came in by the side window and there we met Miss West."

"I see." Miss Maitland sat there for a moment, thinking. Then she turned to Francie. "Now, Frances, do you agree with this story, or have you anything to add? You seem to have something on your mind."

"Yes, Miss Maitland, thank you." Francie spoke in a rush of relief. "Penny hasn't told you half of it because she's being nice——"

"Oh?" Miss Maitland raised her eyebrows.

"Penny didn't know I'd made the date with the boys."

"No more did I," said the headmistress grimly. "I thought I had forbidden, expressly forbidden you to see your young friend without a written permission from your father. Did you not understand my attitude?"

"Oh yes," said Francie, "but I didn't agree."

"You didn't *agree?*"

With anyone less controlled than Miss Maitland one might have said her voice here became a squeak of indignation. She looked really astonished.

"Why, no, I didn't," said Francie, faintly surprised at the effect her words had. "You see, Miss Maitland, I know my father so well that I was absolutely positive I was right. He would have given me that permission. To withhold it just because we couldn't get into contact with him—it wasn't *fair.*" Her eyes met Miss Maitland's squarely. "I'll think *that* no matter what anybody says," she added defiantly. "It wasn't fair."

The headmistress caught her breath, and by some inner process of her mind regained control of herself. No doubt she reflected that this philosophy, though alien to hers, was a widespread phenomenon in Francie's own country. She caught and held on to the temper which had nearly slipped from her grasp. "I will give you the benefit of believing, Frances, that you are not speaking in an impertinent spirit, but I'm afraid you haven't the slightest conception of our way of looking at things. The point is not whether you think a decision of your headmistress is fair or just. The point is that you are still a pupil under my direction, a member of my school. You are expected, like every one of the others, to obey my orders. I couldn't run a school unless my girls accepted this very simple, fundamental idea. Until you are an independent adult——"

"But surely we're supposed to think a little bit for ourselves, at this age? We're not children. Why, at Jefferson High we had our own council meetings, and made up our own student government rules, and everything. Of course there was some control by the faculty, but they *wanted* us to learn to govern ourselves, Miss Maitland. That was the whole idea of education, they said. If Pop were here to explain to you——"

Francie was very much in earnest now, and had long since forgotten her customary awe of Miss Maitland. Her mind was seething with ideas and the urge to explain herself. Her eyes sparkled as she talked. Penny stared at her in amazement. The headmistress's impassive face relaxed a little; her mouth may even have twitched a little, though neither girl could see this.

"I understand," Miss Maitland said, as Francie paused for breath. "I have heard of this system before. After all, Frances, our prefect system helps toward self-government, too. And at Jefferson High, no less than at Fairfields, there are certain fundamental rules which must be enforced by the faculty when the students fail—as you have failed. As long as you were a student here, you should have abided by the rules."

The past tense was significant to Francie. She cried, "Even if I knew you weren't being fair?"

"Even if you *thought* I wasn't being fair," replied Miss Maitland with emphasis. She placed her arms on the desk and leaned forward. "Try to see it from my viewpoint, Frances. Where would I be, where would Fairfields be, if I allowed every one of you big girls to decide for herself which rules she approved and which she did not? Every one of you would run wild in her own way. Of course she would! It's so obvious that even a stupid person would understand, and with all your faults, Frances, I have never considered you stupid."

"We don't run wild at Jefferson High," said Francie, after a pause.

"Whether or not you realize it, Frances, both your teachers and your parents are seeing that you abide by the basic rules. I am in the position of both teacher and parent, at the moment. But that is in any case irrelevant. You—are—*not*—at Jefferson High. You are at Fairfields. It is a fact which you forgot, which is regrettable."

Francie was silent and thoughtful. "You—are—*not*—at Jefferson High. You are at Fairfields," Miss Maitland's voice re-echoed in her ears. Suddenly time turned back, and Francie was in Pop's office on the day of the *Richard the Third* treat . . .

"Don't you ever stop to think you might be wrong, sometimes? . . . Not just tolerance of other people —understanding . . . Getting along with the other fellow on his grounds . . ." Funny, she could almost hear Pop speaking.

A sudden shame overwhelmed her as she remembered with dreadful clarity the whole sorry string of events of the previous day. Yes, Pop was right—and Miss Maitland was right—and she, Francie, was hideously, disgustingly wrong, and stupid, too. Oh, why hadn't she seen it? Of course she couldn't go around making up her own rules as she went along. It was true, Fairfields wouldn't be Fairfields, if all the girls did that. In a flash she saw herself as Miss Maitland must see her—stupid, conceited, always sure she was right—why, just a brat, really! And all of a sudden, now that she was probably leaving, a great liking and respect for Miss Maitland surged up in her.

"Oh, Miss Maitland," she faltered, "I see it now. I was wrong. I shouldn't have done it. I'm—I'm sorry. I should have understood. Pop said I needed to understand——"

Miss Maitland's voice was carefully impersonal. "I'm sorry, too. I must write to your parents this afternoon, I am afraid, explaining the circumstances. It would be impossible for you to remain at Fairfields now. I'm sure you both understand that."

"Oh no! Oh, please, Miss Maitland!" Francie

cried out in anguish. "Please, Miss Maitland, it doesn't matter about me, but——Listen, could I talk to you alone?"

Penny gave her a long look, but Francie would not look back. She kept her eyes fixed imploringly on the headmistress.

"Very well," said Miss Maitland, sighing. "Penelope, you may go into the other room and wait."

The door closed softly behind Penelope. "Now, Frances, what have you to say?" continued Miss Maitland.

"It's about Penny, of course." Francie drew a deep breath. "Miss Maitland, please do think; is it fair, even from your viewpoint, never mind mine, to punish Penny for something she never meant to do? I give you my word, she didn't know she was going to meet those boys. I told her after we'd started out, while we were waiting for the bus."

"Then there was still time," said Miss Maitland, "for her to turn back. No, Frances, I'm afraid——"

"But Miss Maitland, is there a girl in the world who would have turned back just then? Would you really want anybody to be such a horrid prig as that? I know a Sunday-school book would say she should, but it just wouldn't be *human* to do it. It would seem cowardly, too. Don't you see?"

Miss Maitland did not reply.

"I never meant us to go out driving or do all the crazy things we did, like missing the bus back to school," continued Francie, talking fast. "If Penny had known how bad we were going to be—but she couldn't have, because I didn't, myself. One thing led to another. She promised at the beginning that she wouldn't run out on me, that's all, and every time she hesitated I held her to it. It was me—I, I mean—who suggested going along in the car, and *I* put in the telephone call and said we'd be back later, without Penny knowing I was going to do it until after I'd done it. It was I who made every single suggestion. The boys didn't know any better; they didn't know how serious it was; they're only used to the way we behave at Jefferson High. When Penny got scared I reminded her she had promised to stick by, and she kept her promise. How could she help herself?"

"Go on," said Miss Maitland as Francie paused to look at her with pleading eyes. "Is there any more?"

"Yes, there is. Lots. I know you might say she shouldn't have been so weak as to go along all the way, but listen, Miss Maitland. This expulsion will ruin Penny's life. It's not just a regular expulsion. I'll tell you. She's been worried and unhappy lately because. . . ."

Eloquently she described the situation at Penelope's home, not sparing Uncle Jim or the fate which had seemed to be closing in on her unfortunate friend even before this disastrous episode took place. As she talked she could see Miss Maitland's interest growing. Francie had never been so persuasive in her life. She was inspired clean through to the end.

"Why have I never heard of this before?" asked

Miss Maitland when she had thought it over. "I should have thought that in an affair of this sort, any one of my girls would have come to me."

"Oh, Penny would be afraid to come to you. We're all terribly afraid of you, Miss Maitland. Not me, of course, not really, but the others."

Miss Maitland's mouth twitched again at the last sentence, but she grew grave as she considered the rest of the speech. "I should regret it if anyone else carried reserve to such an extent," she said, half to herself. "Perhaps if I—but never mind for the present. I think," she said, standing up, "that this situation needs more thought. I agree that we must not be hasty to condemn Penelope. For the rest of the day, you and she may be together in your rooms upstairs while I ponder all of this information you've given me. Oh, by the way, a letter has arrived for you, and Ella wasn't sure if she should give it to you, under the circumstances. I think I must ask you to read it here, in my presence, as it may possibly be from your young American friend."

But it wasn't; it was a note from Aunt Lolly, saying that she had come back from Ireland, and asking Francie for a weekend soon.

"Whee!" cried Francie. "The Marines have arrived! I mean—oh, do please excuse me, Miss Maitland, but my Aunt Lolly is back in England and if anybody could talk this over with you, it's her. Aunt Lolly—you know, Mrs. Barclay, my godmother; Pop told you I could go to visit her any time, remember?"

"Yes, I do remember, but under the present——"

"I don't mean I want to go now, Miss Maitland," said Francie, interrupting in a way that would have scandalized the other Fairfields girls. "But she could come here, you know. She would, like a shot, if you'd let me call her up. Or why don't you, yourself? Do, please, Miss Maitland, and do please see her before you write to Penny's mother, because honestly Aunt Lolly understands about Penny and all that. We told her in the holidays, and she talked to Penny's mother then and managed her beautifully. Aunt Lolly is——"

"So you think she will manage me beautifully as well?"

"I don't mean it that way," said Francie, laughing a little. "I don't care for myself about being expelled. It's Penny I worry about."

Miss Maitland looked at her curiously, and then smiled. She actually smiled. "Very well, I'll talk first to Mrs. Barclay," she said.

The girls never did figure out what Aunt Lolly did, exactly, to commute their sentence. Even Francie didn't have enough faith to presume that her godmother was powerful enough by a wave of her wand to save not only Penny from her undeserved fate, but Francie from her richly deserved one.

Aunt Lolly knew, though. She wrote to Pop about it.

"This is to report to you," she wrote, "the storm

which has blown up and subsided in the teacup of Fairfields School. Your daughter was very nearly expelled and sent home to you, presumably to the hotel in London if not to Iran, in blackest disgrace and I must say, Fred, that it's a miracle the matter has died down as it has. I don't consider that Francie, given her very different background, was really such a wicked child as appearances made out. These are the facts . . ." and she gave them to Francie's father very clearly and succinctly, so that he would see the picture for himself. Then she continued with her own part in the affair.

"In response, then, to a frantic summons I went to Fairfields to do battle for Penny. Francie, and this is a triumph, recognized how wrong she was and didn't expect any letting off. At first I must admit that my heart nearly failed me, because that Maitland woman is a redoubtable female if ever I saw one. Closer acquaintance reassured me. She's a really fine person, human and understanding, and she does a wonderful job at that school.

"It seems Francie amused her vastly by suddenly going on the warpath and standing up for herself in a way that Miss Maitland obviously considers a novelty. English girls are very spirited, given certain conditions, but their ways are not Francie's, it seems. Miss Maitland says that it was a new experience for her, and as soon as she realized that the child wasn't being 'cheeky' she made a genuine attempt to understand the barbarian philosophy! Then, when Francie honestly realized and admitted how wrong she had been, that softened Miss Maitland further. However, if you ask my opinion, the thing that appealed to her most was the fact that she exhibited a virtue which an Englishwoman could recognize from the start. Francie was loyal in her plea for her friend Penny, and shouldered all the blame, as of course she should have done, without question. And she expected no quarter for herself.

"So much for Penny; Francie saved her friend. The unhappy situation at home carried a lot of weight when all was revealed. But as for our little girl herself, Miss Maitland tried to be adamant. Given *only* Francie, she kept saying, and a whole school full of girls like Francie, or with Francie's brand of parent, she would consider some punishment short of expulsion sufficient, but she had all the other parents to think of. What if word got around that there had been such a flagrant breach of the rules? The whole reputation of Fairfields was at stake. She couldn't afford the risk.

"I argued that Francie's nationality ought to save the name of the school if nothing else did. To know she's American is to forgive a good deal. And Francie isn't a real Fairfields girl from way back; she's a recent arrival. I had to talk bluntly, as hints won't do with a woman of Miss Maitland's type, and in the end I was successful. She still worried, she said, that the example might have been set, but since Francie had been caught out, this fact along with a rather spectacular punishment might take the place of expulsion. After all, no headmistress likes to admit complete failure . . . So Francie stays, though at a price. She is not permitted to pass through the school gates again until the end of term, and must miss whatever 'treat' her form may earn for good marks, including journeys to the beach for a day's bathing. Serve her quite right, I said, speaking on your behalf as well as my own. I am sure you'll agree.

"I was then permitted to interview both culprits. Penny looked far more woebegone and guilty than Francie, who was simply radiant that her sins had not been visited on her chum's head. But that is what life is like; justice is always being blurred by the vagaries of human nature. I wish we could do something for that other child. It's an unhappy situation altogether."

Pop cabled Aunt Lolly, "GOOD JOB VERY GRATEFUL COMING BACK NEXT THURSDAY."

CHAPTER 12

"Penny! I say, Penny, come and look. Do come!"
"Can't you tell me? I'm so busy."

Except when she was hard at work, Penny's temper was angelic, but she had reason to be distracted now. It was only natural that Francie's demands should irritate a producer whose play was just about to begin its one and only performance. In fact it should have begun already, but like most amateur productions it was late getting started. Out in front, sitting on hard benches in the Hall, the parents and special friends of Fairfields girls, who had come to school for breaking-up day, were not surprised or, as yet, impatient. They had already been through a great deal. The *Dream* was the last, most important event of an exhausting program which had begun in the morning with the singing of the school song and had proceeded by way of various exercises—riding, gymnastics on the lawn, recitations in French and a few musical offerings—to this, the deferred climax.

For the past fifteen minutes the curtain had been due to go up, but Penny was still hard at work on the last touches. Just as she put Hippolyta in place it was discovered that her gown hung down too far on one side, and while that was being stitched, somebody upset a pail of water on the platform, obliterating the chalk marks which were so important to show the little girls where to stand. It was all very well for Francie to be airy and carefree and thrilled, where she stood peeping out at the public from a vantage point near a crack in the curtain. Francie's scenes were finished and complete, for better or worse; it was Penny's job now to arrange them.

"Oh well, never mind," said Francie in placating tones. "The thing is, your people have come in with mine and they're sitting all together. I can see Aunt Lolly as plain as anything, and Pop next to her. I never thought I'd be so excited." She hummed and danced a little, standing in place near the crack. "There's Jennifer's parents just coming in and sitting near the back, I guess so they can escape quickly in case they get bored. Mrs. Tennison is wearing the most ghastly hat you ever saw in your life."

"Shhh! Jennifer was around here just a minute ago," said the startled Penny. "I can't think what's got into her—she's been wonderful with the little girls lately. I never thought to see Jennifer Tennison go in for art."

Francie smirked modestly. She knew it wasn't a respect for art that had entered into Jennifer's soul. That day at rehearsal Francie had belittled the very foundations of Girl Guidism and Jennifer had seen to it from that moment on that the fairies learned the meaning of Discipline with a capital "D." There had been no more rebellion in the lower ranks, much to Penny's astonishment and Francie's amusement.

"Everything looks perfect, simply perfect," she declared. "Shall we ring the curtain up, Penny? I'm afraid they're getting a wee bit restive outside."

"Here comes——" said Francie, her back to the stage. Penny gave a hoarse cry of rage.

"Do go out to the audience, Francie, and get out from under our feet. Go and sit there for this opening scene, why don't you? Report on how it goes. That way you'd be of some use."

"But don't you need me here?"

"I need you more out there," said Penny. "Anyway, step back from the curtain. We're beginning."

Obediently Francie slipped off her smudged smock, and in an unadorned green tunic went out to join Pop and Aunt Lolly. The curtain did not go up immediately, in spite of Penny's optimism. From the front, Francie could see mysterious bulges which appeared and disappeared behind its folds, and heard mysterious bumps and shuffles.

Her godmother and father greeted her in kindly fashion. "Does your appearance mean something's going to happen soon?" asked Pop. "Because this bench is just a bit narrow for comfort. Not that I'm complaining."

"It can't possibly be much longer. Poor Penny is standing on her head, practically." Francie broke off to nod and smile at Penny's mother and dark-eyed Uncle Jim.

"We're wondering when you get your final report," said Pop. "Just been talking it over. Are you going to cover the Nelsons with glory, do you think? A good report would be a nice thing to show the State U. examiners at home when the time comes. I suppose you've already thought of that."

"Sure I thought of it. Why else should I have worked? What do I get, Pop, if the report's a bad one?"

"A beating, naturally," said Pop.

"But if it's good, on the average, I'll still get that coat, won't I? Or does you-know-what put me out of the running for that?"

Pop looked puzzled for a moment. "I know what?" he repeated. Even Aunt Lolly laughed.

"My disgrace, silly," said Francie. "My moral leprosy. My wrongdoing. Or have you forgotten that I've been sent to Coventry, practically, these last few weeks?" She lowered her tone so the Stewarts would not hear, because Penny had never confessed to them about the row. Then, remembering that her neighbors must not grow suspicious of all this whispering and murmuring, she spoke aloud in a cheerful tone, "I'll bet you don't know where that expression came from, about being sent to Coventry. Do you?"

"No," said Pop.

"No," said Aunt Lolly after thinking a little. "I thought it was on the tip of my tongue, but I guess it isn't. I'm sure I used to know, but I've forgotten."

Francie sighed. "Education's a wonderful thing, I don't think. Really, you Americans! Well, since I must tell you, it was this way. During the civil wars of the seventeenth century. . . ."

It was not a very interesting story, but Pop was proud of Francie just the same. It was nice to think his daughter knew so much history, he said.

"It ought to knock them for a loop in Jefferson when they find out. What do you think, Laura?"

"Oh, there's no doubt about it; Francie has learned a good deal at school." Aunt Lolly smiled in an understanding way at Francie, implying that her goddaughter had learned a lot more than a mere knowledge of seventeenth-century civil wars.

From the piano up near the platform, the opening chords of a march suddenly sounded. Francie recognized it for the curtain-raising piece, and settled down to watch the performance at last. Jerkily the curtains drew back. From this angle the scene looked fairly nice, she told herself, and she was suitably gratified by the spatter of applause offered by the audience.

After the first lines were spoken and she could relax, she had time to notice, out of the corner of her eye as it were, that Aunt Lolly seemed very chummy all of a sudden with the Stewarts. She was sitting next to Uncle Jim and they had their heads together, actually, and were talking away like the best of friends. How odd! How could Aunt Lolly bring herself to be civil to that awful man? It was very puzzling.

With a start, Francie realized that the second scene, where her presence was required, was approaching at a pretty good pace. She ran backstage to report for duty, and to make reassuring comments to Penny and Miss West.

It was when she was on the stage as a member of Titania's train that she noticed something new about the audience. Somebody was sitting in her place, near the end of the bench next to Pop. She stared at him indignantly, feeling that Pop should have put up a fight for that seat, and then she looked again, incredulously. The boy had turned his head away and for a moment she saw only an ear and a side view of a crew cut. Then he turned back to face her. It really *was* Glenn. She nearly squealed outright in amazed joy.

"By paved fountain, or by rushy brook,
 Or in the beached margent of the sea,
 To dance our ringlets to the whistling wind," said Titania.

It was Glenn, there could be no doubt about it.

But how? What had happened? How had he known enough to come today, at the one time when he'd be sure of welcome at Fairfields? Francie had never attempted to write to him after the debacle of the forbidden date, though she had received various postcards from the Continent—pictures of the Champs-Elysees or the Vatican. As part of her punishment, Miss Maitland had censored all her mail, a practice which had a chilling effect on her desire to write letters.

Francie was so staggered by the sight of her friend that she completely forgot to care that she was in a play. Until that moment she had been admiring Penny for the smooth way the performance, after its late start, was clocking along. No one had yet gone up in his lines, and even the smallest girls were well drilled, thanks to Jennifer; but now she didn't care a bit for that. She was only eager for the scene to come to an end, or at least for Titania with her attendants to leave the stage to Oberon and Puck, so that she herself might be at liberty for a few moments.

At last she was free to squeeze around the side of the curtain as quietly as possible, run down the corridor and get into the Hall near her family's bench.

"Glenn!" she called in a whisper. "Glenn!"

He turned his head and smiled at her. Hesitating at first, he plucked up courage at last to slide out past knees and over feet. Just outside the Hall he met her with an eagerness equal to her own.

"Wherever did you pop up from?" she cried.

"Oh, Italy. I was in Spain too for a couple of days, after France. We had a swell time in Spain. Wish I could have stayed longer, but Bob had this boat to catch, and after that I was at loose ends, so——"

"You didn't have a very long time, after all."

"No, I guess not, but it's no fun poking around in a foreign country on your own when you can't talk the language. Say, listen, Francie——"

"How do you happen to be here, though, at Fairfields?"

"Well, I never heard from you and I figured something might be wrong, so I sent a wire to your Dad and he invited me today. I just made it in time. I couldn't catch the same train as his, but he knew I'd turn up. We figured on surprising you."

"Well, you did, all right. It was a swell surprise."

"Glad you think so," said Glenn with a sudden touch of formality. They were both quiet until he said, "Now listen, about this trouble I got you into, why didn't you let me know? You didn't have to face it all alone. Maybe I could have helped out. I can't tell you what a heel it all makes me feel. Why, you might have been expelled, your Dad told me. He gave me quite a bawling-out."

"He shouldn't have. It wasn't your fault at all. It was mine for not telling you in advance about the rules."

"But if it hadn't been for me——"

"Oh, skip it. I wasn't expelled, anyway," said

Francie, looking down at her feet in their gilded ballet slippers.

"How's Penny? Bob will want to know."

"Penny's fine. You know she directed and produced this show, the whole thing. Did you know that?"

"No kidding! It's a good show, too, lots better than most of these things I've seen. You looked awfully nice up there on the stage yourself, Francie."

Another awkward silence fell.

"I don't have much of a part," she said at last.

"I know; your father said you designed the scenes and all that instead. Between you and me, I think you girls are wonderful, putting on a show like this. Everybody's saying how well it goes and how sort of unusual the stage sets are."

"Really, Glenn?" Francie's eyes shone. "Oh, that's wonderful."

"It's not only me who says it. I've overheard some of them."

"Well, of course everybody has a daughter or a cousin or something in the performance, which makes a difference." She tore her attention away from Glenn to look at the stage. "Goodness," she said, "I've got to get back, but quick! I'll come out again as soon as I can. 'Bye now."

Francie found Penny deeper than ever in the intricacies of her work, inclined to show bad temper with her until she told her news.

"Guess what! Glenn's come back!"

"Glenn?" Penny stared in disbelief. "You mean he's out front now?"

"Look for yourself; he's sitting on the same bench as your mother. I'm sorry he couldn't have brought Bob as well, but Bob had to go on with his father to the States."

Penny giggled mischievously. "What a good thing Miss Maitland never saw him. She'd have a fit if she knew, wouldn't she?"

They heard Puck saying on the stage, "Fear not, my lord, your servant shall do so."

"That's our cue. Both of us. Come on!" cried Penny, and they abandoned gossip to hurry onstage as the curtain fell. Francie had to see that her trees were shifted to a new position, to denote *Another part of the forest.*

A Midsummer Night's Dream is a long play. Usually when it is put on at a school it seems longer than ever. There are all the Fourth Form fairies who must do their special ballets, and so on. But that afternoon it didn't seem as long and boring as usual; the teaching staff admitted it happily among themselves. When Puck made his curtain speech,

"Give me your hands if we be friends,
And Robin shall restore amends"

a large proportion of the audience was pleasantly surprised to discover that they were actually at the end, and that little Jane or Susan had not after all disgraced herself.

Backstage, Penny was a nervous wreck, but Francie rushed out again to meet Glenn.

She interrupted a scene she could never have imagined in her wildest dreams. Glenn, in company with her father and Aunt Lolly, was in animated conversation with Miss Maitland, of all people. The headmistress turned to greet her as she approached, and she was actually laughing.

"There you are, Frances. As you see I've made the acquaintance at last of your young friend. He has behaved beautifully, and apologized for everything."

Francie glanced in wonder at Glenn, who blushed. "I'm glad," she muttered, confused. "I always thought that if you'd really met him you mightn't have worried."

"All's well now, at any rate," said Miss Maitland, "and before I go, I must congratulate you on the stage sets. They were really excellent. You showed a genuine understanding of your work. Didn't you think so, Mr. Nelson? We're all very pleased with Frances this afternoon."

Mr. Nelson looked exceedingly gratified. "She's always been good at art," he admitted.

"I hope she won't forget about it when she returns to your home. We have two very talented girls in this year's finishing class. Penelope's direction was remarkably good, I thought," said Miss Maitland, "and I must hurry now to tell her mother what I think of it."

"Oh yes, Miss Maitland," cried Francie. "Do lay it on thick, won't you?"

The headmistress gave her an understanding nod

and disappeared in the crowd. Pop looked after her. "She turned out to be quite human, after all," he said. "Well now, kids, what's next on the program?"

"I thought Aunt Lolly might like to——" began Francie, but Aunt Lolly shook her head, smiling.

"Whatever it is, it must wait. I too must talk a little more with Mrs. Stewart, as soon as Miss Maitland has finished," she said. "Suppose we meet at the front door when they're serving tea to the parents."

"That's queer," said Francie, as Mrs. Barclay went off. "I shouldn't have thought Aunt Lolly would be so enthusiastic about Penny's people."

"Your Aunt Lolly always knows what she's doing," said Glenn. "Shall we go on and find out where all the people get those cups and plates?"

"Yes, let's."

"Oh, Francie, *Francie!*"

Penny came rushing through the tea-drinking throng, forgetful of them all. She was wildly excited and happy. She threw herself on the wondering Francie, so that tea splashed from Francie's cup and Glenn had to leap to the rescue with a pocket handkerchief. Pop just looked on and grinned.

"Whatever is it?" asked Francie, somewhat indignant.

"I'm sorry, but it doesn't matter. Francie, it's all fixed, isn't it wonderful? Your Aunt Lolly is a magician, absolutely. Oh, I've never been so happy in my life!" She squeezed her friend rapturously, and more tea was splashed.

"Now wait a minute. Glenn, would you mind holding this? Thanks. Now, Penny, explain."

"I'm going in for stage work!" cried Penny. "I'm going right on to a dramatic school as soon as the summer holiday is over. There's no more danger of secretarial school. Does that explain everything?"

"But your Uncle Jim——"

"It's all right about Uncle Jim. He's convinced. He's been talked over. He—I know it sounds like boasting, but I think he's actually proud of me, Francie. It was Miss Maitland who began it, telling him how good she thought the *Dream* was, and some other people said so too, and on top of that just when he was beginning to wonder if he hadn't been wrong all along, your marvelous Aunt Lolly came along and finished it somehow. I don't know exactly how she did it, but Mummy says she was incredibly clever. And Francie, I'm going back to the States! It's Mrs. Barclay again who did that. She's written to a friend of hers in New York and it's practically settled already; I'm getting an exchange scholarship in a New York school for a whole year. I can have my holidays with you. I think I must be dreaming. I think it's a wonderful world. Pinch me, so I can be sure I won't wake up."

"Penny!" Joy rendered Francie almost speechless. At last she gasped, "And to think that just a few weeks ago——"

"I know. Whoever would have thought it?"

Little by little the crowd drifted out of the Hall

FRANCIE

and away from Fairfields. One by one, cars drove up to the great door and carried off girls, parents, and luggage. The big old house grew quiet. The last party to leave was Francie's. In the taxi she twisted around to take a farewell look as they rode off, down the drive.

"Tired, chicken?" asked Pop.

"Not yet. I'm still too excited." She sighed and leaned back against Glenn's protecting arm. "Oh, what a splendid day! Aunt Lolly, if you hadn't ever done another nice thing in your life, you'd go to Heaven just on account of Penny."

"I'm glad if you think I helped," said Aunt Lolly in a modest little voice. They all laughed.

"Pop," said Francie suddenly, "about that fur coat——"

"Yes? I guess I've lost out on that, all right," said Pop genially. "What's it going to be? I can't afford sable, remember, but anything a little more within reason——"

"I don't want sable or any fur coat. I want the money you'd have spent, instead. I have a special use for it."

"What's that, honey?"

"Well, it's for Fairfields. Dear old place. I never thought I'd be feeling like this, leaving it, but I do. I actually feel *sad* . . . I thought if you gave me the coat money, Pop, in American dollars, I could send things here to everybody I know. You know—parcels. I'd send the first one to—can you guess?"

252

"Miss Maitland?" guessed Pop.

"No."

"Penny?" said Glenn.

"No, silly. Penny will be coming to America; she won't need parcels."

"The games mistress who had concussion?" asked Aunt Lolly.

"No, I'll do all that too, of course, later, but my first parcel will be for Jennifer Tennison." Francie chuckled with deep satisfaction at the thought. "It will make Jennifer perfectly *furious* to get a parcel from America," she said contentedly.